The Bedroom Without a Door

J.L. HOLLIS

The Bedroom Without a Door

The Bedroom Without a Door
Copyright © 2022 by J.l. Hollis. All rights reserved.

Additional Copies:

www.amazon.com
www.barnesandnoble.com

Published in the United States of America

ISBN paperback: *9781956895261*

DEDICATION

This book is dedicated to my father, who gave me the "curse," and with whom I wish I had more happy times to spend. To my mother, who was way ahead of her time, and who taught me how to be a mother and a teacher. To my children, who continue to amaze me with their confidence, love and support. And to my husband, I say, "Thanks for always telling me how pretty I am!"

INTRODUCTION

This book was written to give hope to those who feel vulnerable and defenseless and who have no sense of self. Anxiety and pain, although overwhelming at times, can be confronted and treated. Depression and eating disorders can become a part of the past; a rebirth to a new, more productive life awaits. Learn to get out of bed every day and live, love, and laugh. I did. This is my story.

CHAPTER ONE

I sat next to my father on the sticky leather seats of the gently used, coffee-brown Buick as he drove me to Kara's house for my first visit. Although he was silent, he radiated worry and disapproval, and the stale odor of the car coupled with his frown made me feel like I was going to throw up. I longed to have a relationship with him, to feel protected, and even this forty-minute car ride let me down. Dad insisted on driving me to spare my mother any more heartache than she was already feeling. "I'll take Leslie," he insisted, "because she's in no shape to drive herself."

It was 1981, the year that life blew up in my face. I was eighteen. I could not get out of bed in the morning, and I cried practically all the time. If I had the guts, I would have ended my life numerous times. The hurt and sense of worthlessness paled in comparison to death. Kara lived in Port Washington, Long Island, and was apparently the best psychotherapist around.

We walked around the side porch to the back entrance. It was a balmy September morning, and huge old hydrangea bushes lined the walk and burst with pastel colors. My father's gait was laborious and intense, and his six-three frame could not speed up despite the rush of adrenaline that must have been pumping through his body. The waiting room was yellow and inviting, with rows of fresh flowers on the table and placed on the floor by the open french doors. Boxes of children's games added splashes of color to the room. A chill ran up and down my spine.

Together we sank into the blue, corduroy couch, side by side. The silence permeated the room, and I was sure that I had disappointed him. I always did. And he was rarely happy about anything. He said nothing, but his face reflected the silent worrying that I knew well. I needed to talk but not with him.

The door opened with a soft creak, and Kara appeared. She was tall and powerful, with a flowing lavender dress that accentuated the décor of the world that I was about to enter. Her hair was soft and feminine, blonde with a touch of gray, in an updo that was loosely gathered at the back of her head. As my father shook her hand, she thanked him for bringing me and said that we would return in about fifty minutes. With her European accent, she sounded like a softer version of Dr. Ruth. My father returned to be swallowed by the blue sofa, and the door closed gently behind me.

Kara asked what brought me to her office, and I could not put an answer into words; the only thing I was sure of was that life was not supposed to be characterized by constant pain, a longing to be accepted, and anxiety and worries that made it difficult to function. I was a time bomb ticking away, imploding with distress. She promised that, although not an easy ride, together we would come to understand the basis of these feelings, starting with my childhood. Trust being an issue, I was not entirely convinced that it was possible, but life had become so unbearable that there was nothing to lose.

The session ended in a heartbeat. I would return the following week on the same day, at the same time, and she looked forward to working with me. When Kara opened the door, she thanked my father again. "You have a very strong daughter," she added.

CHAPTER TWO

I was always the last one in line, the tallest in our kindergarten class. And that was okay with me, I told Kara. Nobody behind me could comment on my clothes or pull my hair. But then, one Monday, Mrs. Smith changed all that by announcing that from now on, we were to walk side by side in boy-girl pairs. I hadn't trusted her before—or any adult, for that matter—and this only proved me right. Now, I was going to have to ask a boy to walk with me. I climbed to my favorite perch on the monkey bars and eyed the rest of the class at recess that afternoon, dismissing one boy after another. Billy, red haired and rude, had tried to stick earthworms down the back of my shirt already. Carl smelled bad. Jeremy followed blonde-haired, blue-eyed Amy around like a puppy. Finally, I decided on David, dark haired and very quiet. He seemed like a safe pick. Just as Mrs. Smith blew the whistle to go in, I grabbed my courage with both hands and marched up to him. "David, will you walk in line with me?" The words tumbled out in a breathless rush. "You don't have to hold hands with me or anything."

"I won't walk with you!" he cried out with horror. "You're too tall."

Crushed, I would be right at home with those words for a long time to come.

Elementary school became an extension of home, an unsafe place. The sickly, pale green of the walls and the cafeteria smells mixed with that of Elmer's glue surrounded my inner emptiness on a daily basis. All I seemed to hear from the kids at school were cruel words, and I continued to be the target because I did not speak up for myself. I only turned away and hoped that they would stop. "Leslie's so tall she's like a giraffe. She's ugly."

It was just like with my sisters at home. The mean words, the mockery, and the embarrassment that went unnoticed by my parents. At school, my only hope came from watching the clock and counting the minutes until I could go home, to the other battlefront. Although equally disturbing, I could go to my room and be alone, out of the line of fire.

My redbrick childhood home, built in the 1950s, had been weathered by time and the elements of nature. The house was rundown, and thick-branched arms of neighboring oak trees hovered over the roof. It was cozy and charming though not very comfortable.

The red moldings in my room outlined the salmon pink walls like the pages of a child's coloring book. The carpet was a Crayola burnt-orange, seventies shag. My room was in the farthest corner of the house, and part of the chimney passed through in an effort to touch the sky. We painted it white, but despite numerous coats, the imperfect complexion of the bricks remained. I collaged it with pictures and letters of inspiration from magazines and friends. They caught my eye every time I woke up, as if to say, "You can make it through today."

My twin bed was placed flush against the left wall of the room, and it was this bed that cushioned my growth from the time my feet were in its center to the day when they nearly hung over the edge. I slept facing the window and anxiously awaited the "good morning" of the sunlight. For years, it announced whether or not it was a beach day and if I might escape to the promise of the ocean. The sandy south shore of Long Beach was only a twenty-minute ride from West Hempstead.

Hidden beside the bed were two doors that opened to a crawl space for storage. Many a night I wondered if I could escape to another world by opening them. If only Rod Serling would appear and take my hand in another one of his episodes of the Twilight Zone. He never did. Only the hurtful words from my sister Mazzy, whose room was separated from mine by a door-less entry, ever entered to touch me.

Most of the time, it was the presence of her silence—like a plague, powerful and deadly. And there was no door to close to shield myself.

Passing through her violet room on my way to the upstairs hallway was usually a chilling experience. The open bookshelves that lined the walls housed books and old school supplies, memories from my sister's happy and popular high school days. Down the hall, I passed my older sister Ellie's private sanctuary. The only single bedroom on the second floor, and the largest, it was bright and sunny, at least in color. Her door was often closed, and I was rarely invited in.

The stairs wound down and were covered in a thick, worn carpet. A coffee color, they told the story of spills and accidents. Most of these had occurred with food in hand, on the way to a solitary dinner in my room in front of the television. Once in my room, I knew I was safe from my sisters, and I was able to be alone with my thoughts.

The bottom of the steps gave way to a modest dining room on the right. Rarely used, it was reserved for dinners with friends and select family. Directly on the left was a door that led down to an unfinished basement, often the site of our amateur roller derbies. The washer and dryer were down there amongst the spider webs and artifacts from lives before mine. Dusty and damp, the basement was like with my inner thoughts. It was a place I carried with me inside, and I was never anxious to go there unless laundry was piling up.

Dreary wood paneling dressed the hallway walls that led to my parents' bedroom and my father's office. His cherry wood desk took up most of the space, as did he. His strong presence was everywhere: in his forceful handwriting on the bills that were scattered on his desk, the meticulous organization of his music papers and notes, and the overflowing shelves, heavy with books from the past. As he was a child of the Depression, writings about World War II, Hitler, and the Third Reich dominated the stacks. Sprinkled in were thoughts from the classical composers.

The kitchen, full of appliances, gave way to the breakfast nook. A wooden counter extended from the wall lined with musical scores. Most meals were eaten here on the run. Behind the stools was my father's sanctuary, with his armchair and television. He rarely went out the sliding glass doors that led to the yard, spending most of his days here with his beloved dogs.

I always had a nagging feeling that maybe I really was adopted. My sisters told me that I was as often as they could, but I never wanted to believe it. But, with them only fifteen months apart, and me trailing four years behind, I was separated not only by looks but also by ridicule. Often mistaken for twins, their natural, golden blonde hair and clear, blue eyes were enough to make anyone jealous. Where did my ash-brown hair and hazel eyes come from?

I was a dental guinea pig. Hours and hours were spent at the orthodontist's office, beginning at age five. I spent so much time there that I brought my lunch and a book to pass the time. My teeth were a disaster, attributable to family genes and years of sucking my thumb. It was a good thing I was the only child who needed this kind of work, because my sisters would not have been able to handle it. I wore every contraption ever designed, from braces and rubber bands to night braces and retainers. Six years was a long time.

Then came the lack of photographs. Baby pictures of the golden girls covered the walls, but there were none of me. I just wanted to see what I looked like as an infant. Each time I went into the downstairs bathroom, the twins stared at me from the bathtub that they shared as toddlers. When I poked my head into the living room, family photos of only four greeted me. Even the family dogs landed a spot in the portraits!

There was no explanation for the lack of photos; it was just dismissed with a sense of insignificance. This had become the running joke of the family. "There are no pictures of Leslie, remember? Not sure if she was even around. Maybe she was left on our doorstep." Roars of laughter would fill the room, and I would pretend that I was amused. Putting a smile on my face was tough. Looking back at this as an adult, and with Kara's aid, I realized that part of my childhood was nonexistent, as if I was invisible. Although it is common in many families to have more pictures of the oldest children, I had no tangible evidence of my being.

The first photo that I found of myself, in an old box that belonged to my mother, hidden in a dresser drawer, was at the age of five. A black and white, I was standing alone against the brick wall on the side of the driveway. There were no other children around, no sisters or neighbors. Tall and lanky already, I wore a miniskirt and Keds, the rage in the sixties. My face already looked serious and worried, as if someone had pushed me against the wall in order to take the photo. I stood with my feet touching at attention.

During those days, children could play in the streets with their friends, at any age, without fear of being kidnapped, but I still stayed close to home. I was proud of being able to ride a two-wheeler at the age of two-and-a-half, though I didn't go farther than my driveway. I was athletic and coordinated, another difference between my sisters and me.

Although I couldn't exactly define the feeling until years later, going outside caused me anxiety. I often entertained myself in my room with Barbie and her friends, creating the kind of home and life that I fantasized about. Barbie had a warm, beautiful home, with a pool, a modern kitchen, and a sports car. She and I lived with a gorgeous man named Ken, a man who loved me and thought that I was the most beautiful girl he had ever seen. There were no sisters in this house.

The television provided hours and hours of escape. In each sitcom and program, I found myself attracted to the character that finally found happiness. I became the girl who was rescued by the police officer, the woman who got married to her true love, or the lady who escaped her villain and then lived the life she had always dreamed of. The end of each show was a huge letdown. Back to the real world.

When I ventured out of the house each day, I wondered if I would be noticed. It didn't really matter who did the noticing or what they took notice of. I craved positive attention, like a compliment for how I looked or an invitation to join in a group activity with the kids on the block. *Maybe today will be the day,* I thought, again and again. After staying out of the house for several hours, pretending to run away, I crawled behind the fake tree in the living room and overheard my parents talking about one of the neighbors. There was no mention of me. I was sure they would realize I was gone the next time I planned my escape.

At age five, I could recall my mother walking me to the bus stop. The noise of her tying the strings of my hood felt overwhelmingly loud. I remember climbing up each monstrous step into the depths of the loud, intimidating, yellow bus. The other children seemed so happy and carefree. Laughter and playful screams filled the air. I was fearful and found a seat by the window as quickly as possible, alone. Initiating conversation with other children terrified me, and I was scared of rejection. It was far too risky to put myself in a situation where I could get hurt. Inside, I longed to be a part of their group. There was no sign of my sisters. What a relief.

Frozen in my seat, I allowed the rest of me to escape from the bus. Passing trees, cars, and homes entertained my thoughts as my mind developed games and stories to pass the time. The jolt of the bus stopping reminded me that we had arrived at school.

Kindergarten lasted three hours and included naptime. Although the pressures of the curriculum were nonexistent, unlike today, I felt compelled to perform. *I better get the answer. I hope she calls on me. Look, I'm raising my hand. Maybe she doesn't see me.* Driven to be better, smarter, prettier—anything better—my inner voice pushed me to compete, even though I lacked the confidence to believe I could succeed.

Mrs. Park was the most beautiful first-grade teacher at Chestnut Street School. And blonde, of course. It wasn't necessary to go close to check out her eye color. Blue. She had a kind voice and a gentle manner, and she rarely yelled at the class.

I wondered how it felt to be so stunning. Not to care what anyone else thought about you, and to walk the way she did, with a confidence and freedom that must have felt like a million bucks. Or as the Visa commercial put it, priceless. Boy, was she lucky.

Going up to the blackboard felt threatening, and turning my back to the class made me feel vulnerable. My heart raced as I attempted to write the answer to the math problem of the day. I choked with anxiety. *Where's the chalk? What if I can't find it? I think I forgot the answer.* Fearful thoughts ran through my mind, and I longed to be back in my seat, in the rear of the classroom. From there, I could eye the white, large-numbered clock and count the hours and minutes until I could board the school bus, go home, and hide out in my bedroom without a door.

CHAPTER THREE

School days came and went like the ticking of a clock. The routine and structure of awakening, getting dressed, eating breakfast, and climbing the high steps of the bus provided the safest parts of the day. I knew I could count on the bright yellow bus to be there for me when I arrived. A seat by the window, with a view of other worlds and lives, was a daily treat.

In the days when children could freely eat peanut butter and jelly sandwiches without the fear of death from allergies, my lunch consisted of tuna on whole wheat bread. Wonder white bread was just not an option in my house; my mother was nutritionally ahead of her time and aware of ingredients even before package reading became popular. I still loved my tuna sandwiches, despite the bewildered looks of my peers at the lunch table.

I preferred salty treats to sweets. This was unheard of at home, as I was repeatedly reminded. "Can we have her ice cream if she won't eat it?" my sisters asked. "She can just have her healthy bread! How boring." But I didn't have to share anything at school. Tuna was simply not appreciated as a culinary delight like it should have been.

As soon as the educational day began, I longed for it to end. *Tick tock, tick tock* went the clock, echoing the beating of my heart. Each minute seemed like an hour as my eyes repeatedly glanced at the clock on the wall. Like one of Pavlov's dogs, my body would jump, and adrenaline would start pumping as soon as that bell sounded. The days passed swiftly and uneventfully—until third grade.

Immersed in a class project, I suddenly realized that I needed to go to the bathroom. Badly. The class was noisy and chaotic, and Mrs. Smith did not spot my hand up as she floated around the room to field questions about the assignment. Not wanting to go up to the front of the class, I waved my hand more vigorously. Mrs. Smith remained oblivious, and my bladder was ready to rupture.

Peeling myself out of my chair, I slithered up to the teacher's desk, where there was a crowd of students waiting for answers to their questions. I didn't hurry, despite my growing physical discomfort. I was too timid to push to the front and demand attention. When my mouth finally opened, the dam burst, and my pee flooded the floor like a horse. My face felt hot and flushed, as did my legs. The room stood still as the other students stared at me with shock.

After receiving a phone call from the teacher, the nurse came in to walk me in my dripping pants down to her office. She handed me a towel and instructed me to take off the pants I was wearing in the small bathroom located in the back of her office and put them in a plastic bag. I did exactly what she asked and said nothing. Her voice remained calm as she called my mother to come pick me up, and I sat with the towel wrapped around me until I could change into dry clothes.

My mother handed me dry pants upon her arrival. From behind the closed bathroom door, I could hear her and the nurse whispering but could not make out exactly what they were saying. I was choking with shame but was unable to formulate words to describe what I was feeling. The ride home was silent. I took a bath immediately and retreated to my room.

My classmates greeted me with smirks and whispers the next day, first on the bus and then in the classroom. The incident was never discussed, not at home or in school. I really didn't mind if the other kids ignored me, just as long as they weren't talking about what happened. But it became an albatross around my neck for a long time to come, and I carried the weight of fear that I would be humiliated for years. That moment always seemed imminent. I was terrified that the students who were in my class in third grade would ridicule me, and the incident haunted me right through to the end of high school.

Fourth grade brought music. Kids started clarinet or trumpet. The flute seemed like the right instrument for me, and I picked it up quickly as my first instrument. It was built like I was, in metal form, and put my long, bony fingers to good use. Though percussion appealed to me, I could not imagine myself making that kind of noise in such an uninhibited way. The flute carried the melody for the woodwind section, and it also carried me into the world of music.

Reading music was like understanding another language. Each stanza created an emotional hiding place, and the time signatures and tempo changes lifted my spirit. There was no misinterpretation in music; each arrangement was defined and structured, and if I could read the music, I could play it without second-guessing myself.

And so my love of music began. From the early, squeaky concerts of elementary school, through the technical, classical pieces in high school, I found perfection and control. It is said that practice makes perfect, and I became living proof of that. My flute was reliable and steady, always waiting for me when I arrived home from school for the daily round of scales and sonatas.

Music touched me and moved my soul. No matter how forceful or animated the music appeared, it was pure in nature. It was there for the taking, approachable and kind. I never felt intimated or defensive, and I immersed myself in its compassion. So did Dad. I often heard his piercing voice first. "Are you out of your mind?" he would shout at my mother after an argument. Then a roar of piano chords filled the living room as music calmed the beast. As my mother attempted to speak calmly and rationally, my father banged out his frustrations on the keyboard. With each note, he became calmer and more subdued. Time and again, I remained in my room, listening until the music ceased, at which time it was usually safe to go downstairs.

CHAPTER FOUR

Dad was an artist in the truest sense; he was intense, sentimental, and volatile. His aura was strong and powerful, and even after he hammered his feelings out on the piano, I tiptoed around until the emotional dust settled. If I kept silent long enough, he would regain control of himself, and the climate in the house would reach equilibrium. I enjoyed hearing him play when the music was happier, and we bonded over our mutual love of music. Dad played clarinet and flute, and we often played classical duets together in the living room.

His beard, well groomed, was by far his most prominent feature. Though black for most of the seventies and eighties, it changed to a distinguished salt and pepper as he aged. Dad could have been C. Everett Koop's twin brother. While the late surgeon general of the Reagan era was warning Americans about the danger of smoking and AIDS, Dad was preaching about his disappointments with the human race, a far more grave issue. Somehow Koop seemed to have the easier job.

Dad's parents were Polish immigrants who met in Brooklyn. Grandma Rose came over to Ellis Island in 1920 in place of her sister, who decided to stay in Poland to get married.

It was a last-minute decision that cost her life. Years after Rose boarded the boat and set sail for New York, the Nazis invaded Poland,

and her sister and the entire family were murdered in concentration camps.

Dad's Jewish name was Mordechai, but he went by Max. He was born in 1925, the only son of Rose and Ian. Rose met Ian, another Polish immigrant, at the corner market that he managed in Brooklyn. Ian passed away right before I was born, but Dad always described him as a kind and gentle soul. By the age of five, Max was musically inclined and stood up to conduct at concerts. He prided himself on the fact that he was self-taught on the piano, but his main instrument was the tenor saxophone. Max adored classical music, but most of his arrangements and original scores had a Latin flair. His private students came to the house to study harmony and theory, and he was able to support his family.

After serving in the army band during World War II, Max changed his name from Hoffman to Hollis. He claimed it was for professional reasons, and that his name was too ethnic and would not be accepted in the music industry. I later realized that his strong dislike for his Jewish heritage was the true reason for abandoning his birth name. He told many stories about his unpleasant memories of his birth religion and the Jewish members of his extended family, and he repeatedly focused on how he was forced to have a bar mitzvah against his will. He often referred to the religion as Jewish voodoo. Max became a successful jazz musician by trade during the big band, or swing era, of the 1940s. He was a force to be reckoned with on the sax, and he blew his horn with many bands and musicians, the most notable being Tito Puente. Dad transformed into another man when he was onstage. A happier one. I loved seeing him perform and come alive, especially when he dedicated his jazz arrangement of "Surrey With a Fringe on Top," from the musical *Oklahoma*, to only me.

Max met Salina at one of his nightclub gigs at New York's Copacabana. She was twenty-three, and he was eight years older. Sally, as they soon called her, was considered an old maid because she wasn't married. Max took her phone number and proceeded to call her roommate for a date, instead of her. Dad made it clear that there were only two anatomical reasons why he pursued her friend. But after several months, he realized that Mom was the one he was interested in and that she was the finer choice. She had not lost interest, although she said he was a jerk for not calling her first, and the two dated for ten months. In New York, like Hollywood, there was always a happy ending, and the two were married in Brooklyn in 1956.

Ellie was born in 1959, the first of three girls. Blonde hair and blue eyes, like her father, they called her the "milk baby" because of her pale skin. Guaranteed stares and "oohs" and "ahs" from passersby from the supermarket to the park, she was a conversation piece. Born popular, Ellie had the world at her fingertips. When my father's wirehaired terrier, Dudley, was allowed into Ellie's room to meet her, he smelled the crib, and after checking her out, he began to growl. Dudley was relocated to the home of a friend, a decision my father regretted for years to come. "Dudley knew," he said repeatedly as he told the story over and over again. We would come to realize that, as dogs and children can sense intuitively, there was an uneasiness about her even as an infant.

Mazzy arrived fifteen months later. Also platinum blonde, her blue eyes had more of a tint of gray than her sister's. The girls were mistaken for twins for most of their lives. They were also called "schickzas" by the Jews that met them—much too fair but guaranteed to fit in because of their unique look.

I came along three years behind Mazzy. Brown eyes, ash-blonde hair, and weighing in at ten pounds, two ounces, I squeezed my way onto the scene. My father used to say that he had three children, one of each. I've never been sure where that left me, being the last one born. I struggled with my place in the family for years to come, as well as with my gender identification, or private sense of being a female. It probably didn't help that my sisters never shared makeup or fashion tips with me as we grew up. As a matter of fact, we did not share much of anything, and I never learned how to apply eye shadow or lip liner the way they did. They shared clothing, although Ellie repeatedly stole items from Mazzy's closet without asking. I did not fit into anything from their wardrobe and kept a simple tomboyish collection. Called plain and boring, I wore it well.

My only memory of playing with my sisters was in front of the Waldbaum's supermarket. We were living in Queens at the time, and I was five years old. I was taking a ride on one of the kiddy attractions in front of the store, sharing the small seat with Mazzy as we went round and round for a mere quarter. Ellie was impatiently waiting for her turn and began grabbing Mazzy's arm as we approached her, and the two had a small fistfight as the ride went around. We were not wearing the seat belt.

The fall was in slow motion. As my chin hit the pavement, I felt a numbing sensation. There was no time for fear, although I took note of my mother's anguish as she scooped me up in her arms and began running down the street. Blood poured out of my face like an open faucet. She said nothing but moved quickly and intently as if on cruise control. My sisters were out of the picture at that point, and to this day I have no recollection of any reaction on their part or where they went. The emergency room of the local hospital was within walking distance, and ten stitches closed the gap and stopped the bleeding. The scar under my chin remains.

Kara asked me over the course of several years if I had any other recollection of playing or interacting with my sisters in a positive, productive way. I could taste the bitterness of the dishwashing liquid that Ellie put in the juice glass one April Fool's Day when I was seven. It wasn't as cold and refreshing as she claimed it was on that unseasonably hot spring day. Other than that, sitting at the dinner table and seeing them make faces at me from across the table was all I could summon up. By the expression on Kara's face at my response, I knew these memories did not qualify.

CHAPTER FIVE

As soon as I was old enough, I became the number-one babysitter on my block. Itching to make a living and to be an adult, at ten years old I was trusted with even the youngest infants in the neighborhood. Maybe it was because I was tall and looked older. Maybe it was because I had a natural bond with children and proved to be responsible and trustworthy. I didn't even put up signs to get the jobs; news of my skills and availability spread by word of mouth. The Feldman family, right across the street, had six children, from seven months to seven years old, and they must have put in a good word for me. It didn't matter what age the kids were, although I felt a sense of pride when I held the babies. They were not judgmental, and there were no hidden agendas with them. I felt valued and loved, and their smiles melted me. It was a good thing I was working because I had expenses and places to go, and I avoided approaching my father for money. After all, I tried my best not to make too many demands, unlike Ellie. I knew Dad would love me better if I didn't ask for a lot, and I was sure I didn't need any help anyway. Not even for food. When I was hungry for a hot dog at the snack bar at the beach that summer, I didn't ask him. He was so proud, I bet. Not that he showed it, but I was sure that he felt proud that he did not have to spend money on me like he did on her. Doing without the hot dog was the least I could do to make up for her nagging. Money was tight anyway. The music business was not as lucrative as it had been in its heyday, and Mom was just beginning to go back to school for her undergraduate degree in education while working as a teacher's assistant.

Babysitting became a lucrative business venture, and I became financially self-sufficient. Word spread quickly of my love for children, and there was no busting this monopoly apart. My schedule was booked solid. I was popular, at least with the kids. And my sisters weren't around to spoil the fun.

Money was rolling in. It came just in time to finance dance lessons, clothes, and all the incidentals that went along with adolescence, including a down payment for Ellie's first car. I was thirteen. It was a Monte Carlo, in a hideous shade of metallic orange that somehow seemed acceptable in the seventies. "She only needs seven hundred dollars. We know that you have it in the bank, so could you *give* it to her?" asked my father. Though this emptied my account in one lump sum, she got the cash, no questions asked. Dad did not have the money to lay out, and she needed to keep up with her friends. I was sure that she would learn to like me over time if I gave her the money, especially because it was the Bank of Leslie that financed her new set of wheels and allowed her to drive her friends all over town. Months went by, and not even a "thank you" came my way. I never got a lift, and the loan was never paid back, despite the cushy job that she and Mazzy had at Westbury Music Fair as usherettes. Dad and I never discussed this again, and I felt guilty asking him for the money back. And his relationship over the years with Ellie was strained at best; I did not want to aggravate him by allowing her to complain about the material things that she was entitled to that he was unable to provide for her. She tormented him for years. Dudley was right. So I needed to step it up and increase my income.

Babysitting was very profitable, but as soon as I could work legally, at sixteen, I hit every store and fast-food joint in town. I was ready for the big leagues and for more cash. The thrill of the interview was a great motivator, and I was able to turn on the charm and the sales pitch. "I'm a hard worker" got them every time. Offers started pouring in.

My fist gig was at Dunkin' Donuts. The donuts did not interest me in the least. I had learned to resist them, just like I had all of the other fattening foods. Being surrounded by women who were constantly talking about how fat they were provided me with the life skills that I needed to never be overweight. I wouldn't let myself get like them. Ever.

Coffee wasn't really my thing growing up, despite the unlimited supply that Dunkin' Donuts provided me, but I found that asking for a cup of java got me into the adult conversations more often than not, and I tried to avoid being in the company of my sisters as often as I could. This was my ticket out. I barely took a sip, even with all of the sugar and cream, but the information that I took in made the bitterness worthwhile. It was my ticket out of the boring world of the kids and into more important topics, such as politics, religion, and people. The best times were when my sisters were not sitting across from me, making grimaces until I could feel my face heat up with embarrassment. For years, I removed myself as often as possible from their mockery and slipped into the adult world, where I fit in, if not physically, then intellectually.

Fran and John were close friends of my parents, and we often spent time with them on Sundays. They lived within walking distance. They were Italian, and my mother used their recipes for sauce and pasta for years to come. I was grateful for that and enjoyed watching them cook and tasting that heritage, even though I was not a member of it. Partaking in, or even mentioning, the Jewish culture was not going to please my father, so I became an outsider to a group that I did not even understand and tried to find my place in their home. I spent many an afternoon at their home and enjoyed their company immensely, particularly since I found a sense of belonging there that I lacked with my own family.

They had lost a daughter to a house fire several years before, and John walked with a cane due to the injuries that he had sustained. He shared a musical background with my dad, and when they got together, they usually talked about the downturn of the music industry and the lack of morality. The rest of the conversations were dominated by topics like the lack of leadership in the American government and the problems with religion in society. They didn't even realize that I was listening, but I was. Though I had something to add, I kept my mouth shut, hoping that somehow they would find some good in society. There was no time to be a kid, and I continued to earn a living and worry about how I was going to help solve the world's troubles.

CHAPTER SIX

Weight Watchers became part of my life and my vocabulary. Every bit of food that my mother and sisters ate was written on a weekly chart, stuck with a magnet to the refrigerator. Each woman had her own record of calories and food groups. Not me. I just observed. They weighed and portioned food on a mini scale. Every morsel of food was analyzed and picked apart, and guilt came with every meal. There was little enjoyment in eating. "I feel so fat. I'm like a beached whale. None of my clothes fit," my sisters would say repeatedly. Stepping on the scale and comparing results became a routine activity. "They're like babies weighing themselves on a scale," Kara would say years later when I brought it up in therapy. "They never grew up, and this obsession with weight and food keeps them bonded."

My father and I remained on the periphery of their dieting cult. I began to have remorse about food, feeling like it was wrong to take pleasure in it, and I watched my body change and develop naturally. Surely I was not being strict enough with my food intake. By my junior year in high school, I wasn't crazy about the image I saw in the mirror. Already five feet, eleven inches tall, I was pear shaped, with heavy thighs, a plump butt, and very little on top. My mother and sisters referred to themselves as the "dancing cigarette boxes," square shaped on top with stick legs. Breasts were nonexistent, and I was lucky if I was a size A. "Where did you come from?" they asked. "Flat as a pancake." Compared to them and their flabby breasts, I was a definite ironing board, and they publicized this fact no matter where we were. I said nothing. I knew they were right.

The more I looked at my reflection, the more I knew that I needed to change. I couldn't become shorter and cuter (cheerleading was definitely out of the question), but there was no way I would allow myself to be this tall and be huge. It was bad enough that I was several inches taller than the boys. But to weigh more than them? Unacceptable.

In the beginning, my goal was to lose just a few pounds. Maybe ten at the most. I weighed about one hundred fifty pounds. It wasn't necessary to keep a log of my food. A bowl of cereal for breakfast, a small sandwich for lunch, and a light dinner of chicken and vegetables. I had learned from the best calorie-counters in the world, so it was easy to know how to limit carbohydrates and fats.

The first few pounds came off easily. By the end of the first week, I had dropped five pounds, but I was always hungry. Going to bed hungry was the worst. But the feeling of control over my body was far more satisfying than the hunger pangs that I was feeling, and I pushed forward.

I knew for sure that I was really in control one night at my best babysitting assignment, with the Feldman children across the street. The hardest part about watching young children was the plethora of snacks that screamed out to me from the cabinets: pretzels, cookies, and ice cream. Hard to believe that parents kept such crap in their home. Weren't they worried about getting fat? If not for themselves, then at least for their children? I thought everyone was.

The noise of my rumbling stomach called loudly, and I longed for that bag of sourdough pretzels on the kitchen counter. The kids were sleeping; nobody would know. I sat in the den, watching TV, and I was ashamed that I allowed myself to even think about giving in and eating them. I could have eaten the whole bag, after all, since I had only cereal for breakfast and one cup of yogurt for lunch. It was a good day, and I had the willpower of Gandhi during a hunger strike. No one in my house could ever hope to achieve that.

No, I wouldn't succumb. I was learning how to live with that hungry feeling, that longing for food. It was like a natural high. Knowing that in the morning the scale would show another pound missing kept me going. As the numbers went down on the scale, it became increasingly easy to control my appetite. I weighed myself every morning, with just a few clothes on in case the scale was wrong. It provided a cushion, or margin of error. I was down to 135 pounds. Fifteen pounds gone. Even better was the attention that I got. "You look great. You look so thin. How did you do it?" Though my sisters didn't say anything, I knew by the looks that they were jealous. Every time I got a compliment, they glanced my way. I could do something that they could not. Maybe I could lose more.

That infamous Dunkin' Donuts designer pink dress with the white apron began to hang loosely on my wiry frame. Customers were suggesting that I start eating the donuts, but I knew better. I smiled as if to agree, but I knew that I couldn't. The closest I got to indulging was to take great pleasure in serving them their sugary treats and a cup of coffee, and I almost ingested the sweet aroma. I even served the ones that shouldn't have been eating that stuff. *Maybe they'll learn better eating habits from me,* I thought.

As much as I loved pasta, I knew that it had to be eliminated from my diet altogether. It was too risky. "I'm giving up macaroni," I mentioned during a car ride to the supermarket.

"I don't know how you do it. Such willpower," my mother said, in front of my sisters, who only glared at me and rolled their eyes. It was nice to see them jealous of me for once. But they would never admit it, and they seldom spoke to me, certainly not with a compliment.

Giving up my favorite food wasn't as hard as I thought it would be. I had sacrificed so much before that this was a relatively easy step in the process of looking my best and having the perfect body. No pain, no gain.

At school, I made sure to fill my lunch tray and hit every section of the food pyramid. Not that I would ever dare to eat everything on my plate. A bite or two of the hamburger, and a spoonful of Jell-O was more than enough to hold me until dinner, with no snacks in between, of course.

"You're wasting away," said Mr. Jameson, our eleventh grade school advisor, during his lunch duty. That was the most he had ever spoken to me. He usually noticed the pretty, popular girls in my grade. The ones that had leads in the school play, were cheerleaders and were smiling in most of the yearbook photos. Like Christy Danes. A senior—blonde, thin, and tall—she made heads turn without even trying.

I watched her strut down the hallway between classes. Poised, elegant, and stylish. Perfectly dressed. Not a hair out of place. "She's a model, you know," my classmate Elena said in typing class. As if I didn't hear her the first time, she had to say it again. "She models." I said nothing but wondered why she felt the need to share that information with me. *A model*, I thought. *What an excellent idea.*

At my height, modeling seemed to be the only option. Might as well put the tallness to good use. Even more reason to continue the dieting. All of the magazines had these skinny minis on the cover. No boobs, long legs, and adolescent boy bodies. I could look like that. No matter how long it took. I targeted want ads in the *New York Times* for auditions and modeling. Someone had to appreciate my height. With an amateur photographer, I paid for a composite of four shots with my specs (height, weight, eye/hair color, and pants/dress size). At each interview, I wondered if this would be the one—my big break into the field. Really pretty girls were strolling in and out of the waiting room on my first audition in Manhattan at Estella's Talent Agency. They had advertised in the *New York Times*, and there was a lot of competition. I compared my body to theirs as they slithered about, calling attention to their perfect, size-zero bodies. *Too short*, I thought. The owner, Estella, pointed out my cuffed pants in front of a crowd of adolescent model wannabes and stated never to go to an appointment in New York with that fashion faux pas. I messed up again.

When I found the cheesecake ad one Sunday, I was sure that this was the one. *Who doesn't like cheesecake? I could be the next spokesperson for Sara Lee,* I thought. Mom and Dad got a big laugh when I showed them the paper. They later explained to me that cheesecake was the synonym for nudity. Needless to say, I was not called back for any jobs that I applied for. My parents did not give an opinion one way or another as to my hopes for a modeling career. We never talked about it.

Exercise seemed like the next logical step in losing more weight. I was down to 120 pounds, thirty pounds from my starting weight, but I had a lot more to go if I was to be considered for a modeling job, despite the constant rejections. Every morning, I began with simple stretches, and then I secretly weighed myself. I wouldn't allow myself to eat until I had finished my morning ritual of exercise, scale, shower, doing my hair, and dressing.

A feeling of panic consumed my whole body when the scale showed an increase, no matter how slight. One pound was enough to cause an anxiety attack and keep me inside the house, hiding from embarrassment. At least some of the stress was alleviated when I stopped menstruating. No more of that temporary weight gain. But it was time to take more drastic measures to get into shape. At seventeen, I signed myself up for a ballet class at the local dance studio.

Ballet dancers have ideal bodies and tremendous discipline and control. Lean and strong, they are fit and toned. Every ounce of my being longed to look like that—so graceful, sinewy, and slender. The unnatural movements of classical ballet seemed odd at first, and developing a turnout not only hurt but also felt awkward. Being a head taller than the rest of the class added to the feeling of uneasiness at the barre, but I was driven to lose more weight and unnecessary fat, so I swallowed my pride. Besides, it wasn't any more distressing than being at home.

On a teen salary consisting of babysitting cash and donut shop dough, I could afford one class a week. I made sure to buy the black tights because they were slenderizing, especially on my thighs, which were the least favorite part of my body. Nothing I could do would tone those soft, flabby legs.

Riding my bicycle to dance class helped to burn those calories and strengthen my out-of-shape legs. It wasn't far, and I didn't have to rely on anyone for a ride. As soon as I could afford to, I doubled and tripled up on classes, sometimes staying at the dance studio for hours at a time, with no break. No break meant no food, although I did allow myself some water in between on occasion.

I readied my bicycle for the ride home one summer night in front of the studio. Having several months' worth of ballet training under my belt, my body was changing and feeling stronger, and there were eyes upon me, probably with envy. As I hopped up onto the bike, I realized that the father of a girl in the class was glancing over at me, as if he knew me. "How are you?" he asked as I flipped my head and short haircut around to face him. I stared back for a moment, bewildered, wondering if I should have known who he was. "Did you make the team?" His daughter elbowed him to cut him off. "Isn't that Jake?" he whispered to her. I rode off as fast as my boyish legs would carry me.

Three children, one of each, I thought as I pedaled. *Do I look like a boy?* I had no sense of gender at that point but knew instinctively that I had to work harder and harder toward having a body that I could feel comfortable in. I hated the one that I was born with.

CHAPTER SEVEN

I remained immune to the allure of artificially flavored jellies, confectioner's sugar, and fried dough for about one year. The day-old leftovers made the rest of my family happy though. The jelly donuts were Dad's favorite.

During one of the late-night shifts, I noticed that the back door was left open. I had never been in the back of the store; the male employees had the responsibility of disposing of the garbage and locking up at night. It was a balmy summer night, and the glow of the full moon was overpowered by the white swastika painted on the fence.

I couldn't help but wonder if that graffiti was meant for me and if I was once again a target. The paint looked fresh against the backdrop of the wood stockade fence, weathered by time and rain. The symbol made me cringe. *Do they even know that I'm Jewish?* I thought. *It's hard hiding something that you don't even understand.* I was told often that I did not "look Jewish." How I wished I wasn't, especially that night.

As the Nazi symbol continued to salute me, I meandered into the back room, where I was greeted by Mike, the manager. *Does he know about this?* I wondered. Always cheerful and talkative, he seemed oblivious to the world around him, outside of donuts, that is. I had heard that he was a born-again Christian, but I never knew what that meant. Did that mean he hated Jews?

When my father picked me up that night at the end of my shift, I could not bring myself to tell him what I saw. Dad had always spoken about his distaste for Judaism, and the last thing I wanted to do was to feed into that. He did not get along with most Jews. This created many uncomfortable scenes with my mother's family, who were orthodox Jews. So much so that my grandfather once called him an anti-Semite to his face. Interestingly, he never denied the accusation. For the rest of his life, he avoided family functions, saying that he did not want any part of the Jewish mysticism.

I was left with a pit in my stomach that night as I lay in my bed, wishing that I had never laid my eyes on that dreaded back fence of the donut shop. *If only I wasn't Jewish. Then I wouldn't have to deal with any of this crap.* But there I was, knowing I had the moral responsibility to defend a group of people I wasn't sure even accepted me, a group of people I didn't know much about.

I started pouring the coffee at six o'clock the next morning with an agenda. Mike strolled in from the back of the store with his phony, pearly-white grin, as usual. After the door swung closed behind the last customer, I asked him if we could talk, trembling on the inside. "Sure. What about?" he said through his smile.

"Can I show you something?" I asked him as I opened the back door. When his eyes met the swastika, his face remained unchanged.

"Oh, yeah," he said. Mike already knew. "Ryan did that. What about it?"

"Mike, did you know that I'm Jewish and I find that offensive?" I asked, trying to convince myself at the same time.

"Really? You're Jewish?" was his answer. "It's no big deal, honestly," Mike continued, pushing his foot further and further down his throat. "Don't take it so seriously!" Why a grown man, a retail manager serving the public, was not concerned about a hate crime sickens me to this day.

"I would like that fence painted over, please," I said as I glanced over to Ryan in the far side of the shop. He stared back with the expression of the Cheshire cat, but his icy blue eyes met mine long enough to make a confession. Blonde and Aryan, he was the poster child for white supremacists. At nineteen, he had the world by the balls, and he knew it.

"Ryan," Mike said, chuckling, "get that thing painted, will you?"

The fence was as white as snow the very next day, from end to end. The swastika and the fact that I was Jewish were never mentioned again. But my days of donuts and coffee pouring were over. Never again. I gave my resignation and left within the same week. My good deed for humanity was complete.

CHAPTER EIGHT

One hundred and fifteen pounds, a thirty-five-pound drop from my original weight, was the turning point. I had stopped menstruating two years from the time I started, at almost fifteen. My pediatrician claimed that it was time for a nutritionist, who recommended a therapist specializing in adolescents with eating disorders.

I met Dr. Rendall in her lavish estate on the north shore of Long Island. Great Neck was a long, fifty-minute ride from home. Her hair was a shocking blonde naturally, and she was far too pretty to be a psychiatrist. The ritzy décor of the therapy room was intimidating, with a myriad of framed diplomas from top medical schools, surrounded by untouchable artwork from Asia. It was larger than the first floor of my house.

Dr. Rendall directed me to sit in the buttery leather sofa directly in front of her armchair. I was anxious to talk but didn't know where to begin. "Do you know why you're here?" she asked.

"I know that I don't feel like a normal seventeen-year-old should," I replied. I held back the tears.

I continued to see Dr. Rendall every week for about six months, until she got to know me better. Then we switched to every other week. At first, my mother drove me, but as soon as I learned how, I drove myself. The car rides alone were much less stressful.

We got to the topic of food after several months of getting acquainted and a daily antidepressant, after she had made her original diagnosis of clinical depression. Dr. Rendall would say that she wanted me to get to the heart of the matter when I was asymptomatic. That was not to say that I was taking "happy pills." Ludiomil would just bring me to the point where I could think clearly and talk. I wasn't binging or throwing up at all, ever, I told her. She really ought to have saved her work for the more serious cases out there.

"So," she would ask, "how do you feel about food? Is it dirty to you?"

"Yes," I would admit, not understanding why or how she knew to ask that question.

At times, her clone of a daughter would interrupt our session. Four-year-old Diana would walk in and bury her head in her mother's shoulder. She was just as beautiful as her mom, also a blonde, though a more natural shade. My mind wandered into her world, living in this mansion. Traveling. I assumed that her father must have been quite a man. She had a ton of confidence, that's for sure. I longed for that.

Back to the food. I wasn't sure why she was so persistent. She was the expert, after all. I came to her for the answers, but she was looking to me for them. It didn't make sense, and many times I left her house wondering just who was analyzing whom. My rides home were often filled with anxiety, and sometimes I left the session in more pain than when I got there.

Like the time we got to the subject of time. Looking at the clock was both my friend and my nemesis. At school, it was the keeper of time until I made my escape from the ridicule. But at home, it was the instrument that kept track of my time on Earth. It was a reminder of how much time I had left, and it was slipping away.

Dr. Rendall asked me to talk more about the concept of time and what I felt like when I looked at the clock. My mind connected to my ninth birthday party, May 16, 1972, when the table was set for a few friends to come for cake and to sing "Happy Birthday." I had been looking forward to that day for months, and my birthday was the only day that I could call my own. My mother was busy in the kitchen, and my father was in his armchair in front of the TV. I could hear the cheers of the New York Yankee fans from the dining room as I stared with excitement at the colorful paper plates and napkins on the table.

"Honey," my mother yelled to my father, "I think you can wake your mother now." Grandpa Ian had a heart attack shortly before I was born, so we never got to meet. Grandma Rose had been living with us for about a year, after selling her apartment in Brooklyn, and the small den in the far corner of the house became her bedroom. She was a superb cook, and when she baked her famous butter cake, the aroma in the house was heavenly. It was already ten o'clock, and she was not up yet.

Dad opened the door, and I saw Grandma still under the covers as I peered in from behind him. "Mom," he said softly. No response. "Mom," he repeated. "It's time to get up." Silence. I crept into the room close to him as he went over to the bed, though he did not realize that I was right behind him. When he gently pulled the blanket off of her, she lay still. He nudged her shoulder and then ran over to his desk, where he pulled the drawers out and pushed them in with frustrated slams. She never woke up.

As the sirens came down the street, I waited in the corner of the living room, watching the clock. The paramedics rushed in with a gurney and lots of fancy equipment. They came out of the den moments later to say how sorry they were, but she was gone. Grandma Rose had passed away in her sleep from a heart attack. She did not suffer. They rolled her lifeless body out of the house, wrapped in a white sheet. In the stillness, not a word was said. All I could hear was the *tick tock* of the clock.

Did Grandma eat too much salt, even though the doctor told her to restrict her diet? Is that what killed her? None of it made sense, and I tried desperately to wrap my head around what had happened on the day that was supposed to be a celebration of my birth. The party was quickly cancelled, and the table was dismantled. My parents, grieving, talked little about her passing.

After I told Dr. Rendall the story, she asked me how I connected my grandma's death with time and food. Grandma ran out of time, and she would no longer enjoy the taste of food. I was running out of time.

"Did you feel guilty that you were going to have your birthday celebration on the day she died?" she asked.

"I knew that it wasn't my fault, but I was afraid that the same thing was going to happen to me. What if I died in my sleep? Would they roll me out on a stretcher, too?"

"Were you comforted by your parents?"

It bothered me that I could not remember. But I couldn't.

CHAPTER NINE

My first time behind the wheel was in my father's beige Toyota Corolla. We ventured out into the parking lot of the local elementary school. It was a dream touching that steering wheel. I held back the longing to step on the gas and drive as far away from that house as I could. Since my New York State Learner's Permit did not permit me to venture far out, I was restricted to the vicinity close to home.

As he showed me the gas pedal first, I heard the words "never," "accident," and "careful" over and over again. "And you need to drive defensively, you know?" he would say. "Because it's inevitable that some idiot is going to do something stupid on the road." The last thing I wanted to do was become that idiot.

Dad let me borrow the Toyota to go back and forth from Foodtown. Working as a cashier, I learned to punch in prices with speed and precision. The position required skill and coordination back then, unlike the simplicity of scanning bar codes.

They say never go food shopping when you're hungry. Try working in a supermarket when you have an eating disorder and are in a constant state of hunger. Each item that rolled down the belt caught my eye. It became a game to create a profile of each shopper based on the purchases. Some lifestyles were all about convenience. Chips, snacks, and carbonated beverages. Then there were the sweet teeth, with everything from chocolate bars to bakery items. Occasionally you would get the gourmet cook, with meats, veggies, and pasta. I was sure, though, that they were all overeaters. My mouth watered at the sight of every bag, box, and container, but my shift had another three hours, and I would not touch a morsel of food until then.

Once a woman ran right in front of another to get a place in my line. It became a huge scene, and the woman who was cut off flipped out. "How dare you take my spot!" she yelled. "I have places to go!" The other woman would not budge. The fight was at full volume, and the frontend manager, also a woman, joined in. "Ma'am, let's not make this more than it—" She was not able to finish her sentence, as the angry customer got in her face and continued to scream. Not very patient, the manager stated, "What's the matter? Your husband didn't come home last night?" The blonde woman stormed out of the store. Guess she hit a nerve.

That same night, I went to turn the engine on. No sound. "Step on the gas, and then turn it on," I said to myself. No luck. The battery was dead. I had left the lights on. I had turned into one of the idiots that Dad had spoken about. *How could I have done something so stupid?* I made sure that I checked and rechecked the lights each and every time I drove the car after that, and I never let that happen again. At all cost, I tried to avoid making a mistake and letting my father down. If I had any mechanical issues, I was more comfortable asking a coworker or complete stranger than him. He did not function well in a crisis, and his nerves usually got the best of him. It was just simpler to problem-solve on my own, without him getting annoyed at me.

Dad used to say that I was the son he never had, and I could tell by his expression that he felt a certain sense of pride in that. It made me happy to make him happy. Baseball games and horror movies were our thing. Nobody else was interested in going, and I was the only logical choice for the hockey games at Nassau Coliseum. When Ellie and Mazzy were working as usherettes at Westbury Music Fair, seeing Diana Ross and Cher for free while earning tips, I was at the J.P. Parisi Fan Club meeting with the local New York Islanders. I didn't want to work as an usherette, anyway. One of Dad's friends in the music business was able to get them those coveted jobs, but it was too "girly" for me. I would never be able to pull off those uniforms. Not that I got any job offers.

I passed my time studying, dancing, and working. No time for a popularity contest. My sisters were just wasting their time on typical adolescent nonsense like going out and socializing. We spent every summer at my aunt Fanny's summer bungalow in the Catskill Mountains. Those were the days when wives didn't work. And on Friday nights, they waited with the children for their husbands to return from Manhattan for the weekend. Ellie and Mazzy went out practically every night with the other teenagers visiting family in upstate New York, and I was never invited to join them. I stuck around with my mother at the pool and in the bungalow, and I never strayed too far from her side. My father never accompanied us; it was too "Jewish" for him, and he could not bear being a part of anything that smacked of Shabbat and synagogue. Too much of a reminder of his unpleasant childhood days.

At night, the mountain air caused a twenty-degree drop in temperature, and we got to sleep with cottony, soft comforters and extra socks. Grandma Eva made the blankets to match the curtains, but it didn't matter how tacky the color patterns were. We were grateful to crawl under the covers and drop to a quick sleep after a long day of sun, swimming, handball, and conversation.

While my sisters came home at one or two every morning (praying to the porcelain bowl on occasion), I was content staying in with my mother, in front of the TV. Aunt Fanny had a tough time understanding why I wasn't making friends. It seemed to bother her more than me. "Why don't you go out and make friends?" she would ask on a daily basis. My mother would just roll her eyes. All I knew was that the grandmas and grandpas of the Catskills seemed to treasure my company and conversation a lot more than the kids. While tots of all ages were running amuck around the grounds, I stuck close and eyed the senior citizens playing their card games and enjoying each other's company. Their faces lit up when I arrived, and I didn't want to disappoint them.

I spent most of my free time by the pool. It was a long climb to the top of the stairs that twisted and turned, with weeds and overgrown grass peaking out through the cracks of the whitewashed cement. As I took each step, I looked down at my huge thighs and hoped that they would firm up. At the top, the fresh scent of Catskill Mountain air greeted me, despite how out of shape I was. Not at an ideal weight, I felt embarrassed at the sight of myself. My eating-disorder state of mind was in charge, and I either covered my ugliness with a towel or quickly jumped into the pool so no one could see how hideous I looked.

Besides swimming, people-watching became a private game for me. It was amazing how many people were overweight. There were all shapes and sizes represented, and all types of swimsuits, from string bikinis to men's Speedos. Some were stuffed into them like sausages in casing, with fat overflowing on all sides. Others had far too much skin on display, much of it worn and wrinkled, and it was embarrassing. There was always one class act, a woman, with an age- and figure-appropriate suit. She definitely did not fit in among the grannies and their quest for youth.

The aroma of the snack bar, with its smell of french fry and burger grease, hung over the chlorine. Grandpa Charlie—"Papa," we called him—didn't say much but always offered us food. "You want an ice cream?" he asked with his Russian accent that never quit despite sixty years in America. That was about the extent of the conversation. Charles came to the States right before the Russian Revolution in the early 1900s, and my mother said he was cold and emotionally unavailable. She was told that she was an "accident" by her own mother, and Papa was not around much during her youth. She was left alone a lot, which my father said was a good thing, as she grew up with a different mind-set. I was not a lover of ice cream, but I thought maybe if I accepted his offer, he would think more highly of me. When he wasn't looking, I dumped the chocolate cone in the nearby trashcan. Papa didn't notice one way or the other, and he did not approve of me any more or less than he did before.

One rainy day, my cousin Leah and I were sitting in the snack bar. I decided to treat myself to a burger, knowing that I would pay with deprivation for the rest of the day. We approached the counter, and I ordered a cheeseburger and a side of fries, which smelled divine. The woman behind the counter explained that it was a kosher restaurant and that meat and dairy were never mixed. As she explained that, she looked at me as if I had just been dropped onto the planet by an alien ship. I didn't understand why. It was the last time I ate there. I couldn't do anything right, not even on vacation. One of the waiters at the bungalow colony stared at me one night as we were exiting one of the corny, Catskill shows, straight out of a *Saturday Night Live* skit with Bill Murray. Those were the days when all the big-name acts headlined in the upstate hotels, before the Hamptons became popular. I had seen him several times during the dinner shift, when he was busy serving, and I thought he was looking my way. It made me feel self-conscious and almost arrogant and presumptuous to even think that I was being noticed. No one noticed me, and no one ever told me I was pretty. So I made sure that I looked the other way when I saw him. After a while, he just made an annoyed face when he saw me. Thank God I didn't show him that I was interested, not that I would know how to do that. It would have been humiliating.

CHAPTER TEN

Like the ticking of my life clock, high school dragged on. The house was infinitely quieter; Ellie was away at Albany State University, and her fights with my father—live, that is— were not happening. Like the time when my dad was chasing her around the dining room table about some nasty comment that she had made during the summer of '82, right after her freshman year. It had something to do with money and how she needed more, as usual. I don't even remember exactly what she had said, but with Ellie, it usually wasn't what she said but *how* she said it. Fortunately for her, he was not the athletic type, so she remained out of his reach. I'm not sure what he would have done if he had gotten his hands on her.

Ellie had a way of making you crazy. About nothing. That same summer, she shot off her mouth at me in front of her boyfriend, Ian. She always had this edge to her, a mean streak, as my father knew all too well. It took him many years to learn the strategy of keeping the conversation away from certain topics to keep the peace. She always had to be right, and she challenged him on practically everything. Mostly about money, of course. And on how he handled his friendships, and the way she thought he treated my mother. Mazzy seemed to stay out of her reach, unless Ellie was caught stealing clothes from her closet. Dad and I seemed to be the targets of her fury, and I felt my blood pressure rising through the roof. When she shot her mouth off at me in front of her boyfriend, my hands went for her throat until Ian stopped me. He was shorter than me but muscular and was able to block my arms. Ian became infatuated with her during their teenage courtship. Poor guy. I guess he didn't know what he was getting himself into. Ian and Ellie married a few years later, and he confessed to me that he wondered why he had stopped me from fighting back after he really got to know what she was all about. Thirty years later, Ellie would refer to this incident and say that I had a rage problem and that their two children were not allowed to come to my house.

Dad would joke around and say that he knew that when the phone rang from Albany, it was Ellie. He could tell by the ring, he would say. It was a call for money. It would've been helpful if she used her student loans for academic expenses, not for a stereo for her off-campus apartment. My father never had enough to satisfy her. He didn't make adequate money, our house was modest, and material things were not handed to her on a silver platter like they were to her friends. But at least he only had to deal with her voice when she was away, not her presence. When he hung up the phone, he breathed a sigh of relief. Until the next call came in.

The comforting silence in the house continued, in part because Mazzy and I stopped speaking to each other altogether. To this day, I cannot even remember why, but it lasted for one and a half years. No interactions, no looking at each other, no words exchanged. No one noticed, and no one asked any questions. The challenge was walking past each other without making eye contact. I became quite skilled at it, and it was a good thing, because it was a tool for me for years to come.

In high school, I channeled most of my energy into keeping up a straight-A average in all subjects. Anything less was intolerable. After walking home from school each day, I would cook some soup, allow myself only a perfectly measured cup, and begin studying. With the exception of Ace, our Airedale terrier, I was usually alone in the house. Sometimes my father was sitting in the den in his worn armchair, but even then, I was still alone.

The breakfast nook, as we called it, offered a stool and a counter to lean on, and I would spread out my books, papers, and pencils. It was never a mess, even when I was working. Disorganization made me anxious, and the control over this space made me feel less vulnerable. As I worked, tired faces from framed scores of old songs on the dark wood-paneled walls glared over at me.

My heart started pounding whenever I was unable to master the subject at hand. The frustration would overcome me, and I would sit, no matter how long it took, until I was an expert at the task I was attempting, whether it was a math problem or a writing response to a reading passage. I was in charge, and I would hammer out an answer that was neat and presentable. During my junior and senior years, I took advanced placement classes that I paid for through Adelphi University, and I amassed about fifteen college credits before I graduated.

Music remained an outlet and a place where I felt successful. The New York State Schools Music Association (NYSSMA) festival took place every spring, and I participated on the flute. From ninth grade on, I prepared one classical piece at the appropriate level, three scales of my choice, and worked on sight-reading to the extent possible. The sight-reading made me nervous; it was the only music that I could not fully prepare in advance. I would not walk out of the judging room without what I considered to be a perfect score, and every year I received an A+. I could not accept anything lower from myself.

The school staged musicals every year and auditioned members of the pit orchestra for the performances. Although I had heard that no freshman ever made the orchestra, I showed up at the audition with a classical piece from memory. Janet, another freshman, decided to join me, but I knew that she would never make it. I tried to be as encouraging as possible, but inside I knew that I *had* to beat her. I watched her play her song, and she had a weird way of rocking to keep the tempo. Her tone on the flute was airy and off pitch, and I was embarrassed for her. I wouldn't let myself sound like that. When it came to my turn, I began playing, heart racing and all. *Don't mess up,* I thought. *No mistakes.* I passed the audition, but Janet did not.

Though it was quite a feat, I had this insatiable appetite to be the best at everything, and the feeling of pride was only short-lived.

The first musical that I played in was *Guys and Dolls*. It was a difficult score, but I held my own, even amongst seniors and professionals who were hired in from outside the district. As I rehearsed, my eyes could not help but stare longingly at the actors on stage, wondering how it felt to be so free and confident. How beautiful the girls looked with their exaggerated stage makeup and hair. And the dance moves. Angie, a senior during my first show, was the prettiest and the most popular. She was a brunette with large, almond-shaped eyes, and people couldn't take their eyes off of her. And she knew it.

The next three years of shows were not as exhilarating. I played in *Kiss Me, Kate*, *Carousel*, and *Cabaret*, but somehow the magic started to wear off. But never the envy. No matter how technically sound I was as a musician, it never compared to the talent and looks of the cast. I even tried out for the kick line team during my senior year, thinking that most of the girls did make that. During my audition, I saw snickers and heard whispers from the girls in the back of the gym. Even the school nerds usually made the team, but not me. I was too busy with SATs and college applications anyway. Their loss.

By the end of my senior year, it was obvious that I had an eating disorder, with a side of depression. Dr. Rendall confirmed it officially. While most seniors were scared to graduate and enter the "real world," I knew I was already there, I told her. My hair was still short and boyish, and she asked me how I felt about my looks.

"Did you feel attractive? Did you feel like a young woman?"

"Well, no one ever asked me to the prom, and the high school yearbook kind of put it all in perspective for me, if I had any doubts. Let me show you." I took out the yearbook and showed her my senior picture. Underneath the picture was the name "Edwin Hollis," my classmate. When I looked at my graduation picture, over and over again, I began to understand why Dr. Rendall questioned me about my femininity. Aside from the Dorothy Hamill bob haircut (and mine was infinitely shorter than this famous Olympic gold medal figure skater),

I was pale, wore no makeup, and looked far from womanly. Gerry, a senior and arrogant beyond belief, was the president of the yearbook committee, and I was sure that he deliberately put Edwin's name under my photo. After all, he was the one who wrote how I would never be at par with my sister Mazzy, in her yearbook, when she graduated three years earlier. I kept my mouth shut and swallowed the pain and embarrassment, but inside I ached to know why no one had challenged him on all of this. It seemed unjust that he could get away with that. Was there anyone in the world who would take a stand and defend someone else?

The college application process seems like a big blur now. I can hardly remember the tedious process of completing each form, but writing the essay was where I could sell myself, pretending to be more confident and self-assured on paper. I was interested in working with animals, and I loved science, having excelled in biology in high school. I sent applications to Rutgers University in New Jersey, Farmingdale University on Long Island, and some other state universities in New York. I read and reread each paragraph, making sure they were perfect and free of error. And when I mailed them in to each school, I lived for the moment when I would receive an acceptance letter from a university, where I would live in a dorm. Away from my family. Away from my sisters. That's what every seventeen-year-old did.

Rutgers University was the most exciting acceptance that I received, and it was the one I had hoped to get into. It was a great school, and when I told my teachers and some friends, they were very impressed. I would study science, pre-vet to be exact. I loved animals and had the grades to handle the difficult science courses. It all seemed so ideal.

I used my own money to buy the things that I needed to go away to school. Laundry detergent, soap, a bucket for bathroom items, towels, and linens. They were lined up like soldiers in my room, under the window that faced out onto the street. Even Ellie made a comment when she showed some of her friends what I had bought. I'm sure she was jealous. She was never as independent as I had become and always relied on my parents for these things. Not me. I was self-sufficient.

We spent many a Sunday at the local flea market, walking the aisles and visiting hundreds of vendors hoping to make a sale. The prices were good, and being late August, it attracted soon-to-be college students. Nothing really appealed to me, and though there were trendy and designer clothes, I knew that I couldn't wear any of them. My sisters had no problem trying on and purchasing all of these garments. There was always a great deal of dialogue about what they looked good in, what made them look chunky, and what flattered their figures. And there were constant comparisons with women who strolled by, asking how they stacked up to them—so much so that the vendors and other shoppers were sucked into the conversations. I always strolled a few feet back and never felt that I had the right to take part in such frivolity.

When my sisters and mother brought me to Rutgers to drop me off, and we took a quick tour around the campus, I felt my heart pounding despite all of the smiles from complete strangers who recognized me as the new freshman in town. We ate lunch at the university café, and the clock was ticking for them to be leaving on the two-hour journey home. Without me.

That night, at the edge of my bed, I cowered, paralyzed with fear. An overwhelming feeling of helplessness took over as I struggled to stay in control. It was just my dorm room. I repeated that mantra to myself as I stared at the beige carpet and natural wooden furniture. Outside in the hallway, beyond my window, animated students seemed to be everywhere, and their unfamiliar voices seemed to press against me as their shadowy silhouettes passed my window. Instead of rejoicing in the music from their stereo systems, I heard only the drums of a primitive tribal ritual. I covered my head with my pillow. My dorm room became my prison cell.

The escalating feeling of panic was difficult to battle, especially as the other freshmen introduced themselves. They were so together, so calm, I thought. *Breathe in, breathe out. Stop sweating.* This was going to be a more difficult performance than ever before. I was definitely out of my comfort zone, and fitting in was not one of my strengths.

A sweeter roommate I could not have wished for, although Snow White was no match for the inner turmoil that had just been unleashed. Lindsay was a New Jersey resident who lived within an hour from the New Brunswick campus of Rutgers University. A nonsmoker and straight-A student, she had an innocence and quiet confidence that I longed for. Once again, I was the odd woman out.

On that sunny September morning, only three days before classes began, Lindsay and I ventured out into the unfamiliar campus frontier. Our explorations uncovered another modern New World of cafeterias, student lounges, and colorful signs welcoming new freshmen. Lindsay seemed to be energized by this outpouring of acceptance and support. It only terrified me. I was afraid that something would happen to me, or to my family while I was not there. There was no way that I would fit in or be accepted, and I was filled with worry.

Our searches were short-lived, and we returned to our boxes and decorations. The chatter and buzzing about continued well into the night, and so did my anxiety. Though I attempted to sit on my hands so as not to call my mother, I made another call in the hopes of soothing the incessant nervousness, which seemed to be mounting by the minute. I knew it upset her when I called and that it displeased my father. It was a just quick phone call though, since Lindsay had strolled down the hallway to the bathroom and would be back momentarily.

Mom's calm and gentle voice reassured me, though in a matter of seconds I realized how homesick I was. "Give yourself time," she said. I heard my father's annoyance and disapproval as he sat next to her, telling her to hang up the phone and let me grow up, not to baby me. I shouldn't have called. The receiver touched down just as my roommate opened the door. She greeted me with a warm and gentle smile. I somehow returned the gesture.

My Academy Award performance was sustained, though it nearly depleted me. I reached to the bottom of my soul on a daily basis, striving to make it through each encounter, social interaction, and academic situation without revealing the panic and worry that was consuming me at every turn. The more trying every scene became, the more adjusted and settled the other newcomers seemed to be. The contrast came into focus, and I knew subconsciously that something was seriously wrong. There was not one moment of any day that I was not frazzled.

Classes began on a balmy Wednesday morning. As a freshman, most of the courses were prerequisites, such as English, math, and psychology. A straight-A student myself, these were no challenge to me academically. My books and supplies were neat and orderly so as to camouflage my emotional disarray. I sat in a tidy row of seats and flashed a fake smile whenever possible so I would appear happy and be left alone. Blending in was tough, and it took a lot of work. I was exhausted. The fact that my calorie intake was well below normal did not help my energy level at all, and it was physically challenging to get through the day.

The charade went on for only three weeks before the gong rang to end my act. Calls home were frequent and anxiety-producing, for both my parents and me. Dr. Rendall recommended that I see the university psychologist at the Rutgers health center. Mrs. Bloch was caring and professional, and I was able to get appointments quickly, but the few visits that I had at her office sparked pain and discomfort. Sitting in her man-eating, cushiony, brown leather chair, I felt like the bottom of my life was caving in. This last effort was too late; the show was over. I knew pretty quickly that I could not handle being away at school and that no one would like me at Rutgers. Home wasn't right, and the dorms weren't right, and I was miserable at both. I couldn't function in either place. At least at home I could keep an eye on my family and make sure they were okay. Fret about them was constant.

By the end of September, I was packing up my belongings and returning home. My parents asked no questions, yet my father knew that my unhappiness was taking an emotional toll on my mother, and this made him furious. Lindsay looked on with her head cocked to one side like a puppy, sad and confused. Residents in the dorm passed by with a confused glance. I made my trek home.

CHAPTER ELEVEN

As soon as I arrived home, I knew that I had made a mistake. I told Dr. Rendall that frequently, and I was angry at her for letting me go in the first place. I did not have the backbone to tell her that. Wasn't she supposed to guide me, to help me make good choices? The glory of coming back to the familiar wore off in about five minutes, and I could see that nothing had changed. And everyone back at Rutgers was getting on with their lives, being successful. Not me. *Oh my God, what have I done?*

I screamed to my mother to come join me on the couch. Maybe she could send me back to the New Brunswick campus, even get in touch with my roommate before she chose someone else to share her dorm room with. When she hugged me, it was comforting only for the minute before my father walked by and glared at us with eyes like daggers. I knew I had to pretend that I didn't need that hug, at least until he walked by. There I was on the couch, in a fetal position, choking with anxiety. The pain was overwhelming, and there was no escape. Arm in arm, the hurting and I floated in slow motion as life for everyone else swirled around me. Passing me.

Sleep was the only answer, the only remedy for the suffering that enveloped me. I could sleep for hours at a time, even after a full night of it. The relief came only when my eyes were closed, but I was greeted with a punch of anxiety in the chest the minute they opened. The self-tormenting was relentless, and there was no hiding from its fury.

My mother's face was pained, and it made me feel guilty. My father's was annoyed. Ellie had graduated and was working in Manhattan full-time, and Mazzy had returned home from Binghamton University to complete her bachelor's degree locally at Hofstra University. My sisters could not be bothered with me. I'm not sure if they even realized I was back. Ace seemed to be excited to see me judging by the rapid wag of his stubby tail at every encounter. If only I had my own dog, like I had begged my father for repeatedly, it would have felt like I had someone on my side, an ally. I asked him every year, insisting that I was responsible, mature enough to take care of an animal on my own, and that I could pay for one myself, like I had done for all of the other extras that I had. Sadly, each year the answer was no. Don't get me wrong, I adored all of the family dogs, from Ace back to Nico, our German shepherd. But to have my own special friend, with unconditional love only for me, was something I could only dream of.

Food was not a comfort but an enemy. All I wanted to do was eat everything in sight, but the fear of putting on weight was still an inner demon controlling me. The hungry longing and household smells of food simmering reminded me of sitting in the middle-school cafeteria when I was thirteen years old, daring myself to buy a package of Lindsor chocolate chip cookies. As I sat at the lunch table, tearing open the crinkly plastic wrap and eying the scrumptious chunks of chocolate, I thought of my father and stopped eating. One bite was all that I could allow. I threw the rest in the trash. But the floodgates were open, and the deprivation that I had endured for so many years took over my body with such force that I began eating everything that wasn't nailed down. It was the only comfort that I could physically feel. The shame came quickly, though.

The questions that came at me by neighbors about why I was home from college so early were hard to bear, and I stayed in the house as much as possible. This was not the kind of attention that I craved. Money was the only motivation and the drive that got me out of bed in the morning. I had to find a job.

I began working at Toys R Us as a cashier. The store was a twenty-minute bike ride away, and the job paid minimum wage. The other cashier's name was Ronda. African American, she greeted me every morning with the smell of her hair products. She was friendly enough but preoccupied with the responsibilities of being a twenty-year-old mother to a three-year-old son. No one else really spoke to me.

The job was not particularly challenging, so I did my best to get lost in the world of toys to pass the time. There were more Barbies than I could ever imagine, all with perfect physical dimensions, blonde hair and blue eyes naturally, and a wardrobe to die for. Society was not ready for the diverse Barbies that are on the shelves now. From the doll to the board game aisle, I created my own kind of fun, alone. Until I had to go back to the frontend register and deal with all of the brats getting toys. The brats were the parents.

The profile of a cashier at Toys R Us was far different from that of Foodtown. Yet I still found myself hungry; hungry for the material rewards of being the child of a family with means to indulge in the pricey, electronic gadgets in aisle six. But mostly, my hunger was for the father that strolled by, holding the hand of his young daughter, whose eyes grew larger at the sight of each flashy box. I had to hold myself back from taking his hand myself and feeling what it would be like to be loved and protected. It was a good thing I had such a sense of self-control, or I probably would have lost my job.

Thoughts of dying became more and more prevalent. They had always lingered, since I was a child, like a black cloud hovering above my head. I was obsessed with the thought of not breathing, of what it felt like to be dead. Maybe it had to do with the day Grandma Rose passed away in our house. One minute she was sleeping, the next she was gone. Woody Allen put it perfectly when he said, "I'm not afraid of dying, I just don't want to be there when it happens." When it would actually happen became my obsession. My life clock kept on ticking. Each moment was engulfed in a panic that made it difficult to be in the present. I would learn in therapy later as an adult that I had spent most of my life not experiencing the moment.

It took about four months to be able to ease myself out of bed in the morning without that intense sense of pain and panic. Dr. Rendall gave me some strategies for how to get through each day, one at a time, as a sufferer of depression. "Be good to yourself, " she said. "If the day seems overwhelming first thing in the morning, then break it down into digestible pieces. For the first couple of days, try to get through hour by hour. Then you can extend that hour into mornings and afternoons. Set goals for each day and try to find things that give you pleasure, like reading a book or going for a walk. Try to find your own silver lining." It was hard to find satisfaction in life when I felt like such a failure, so I focused on getting up in the morning, showering, getting to Toys "R" Us, and returning home in one piece.

By that time, I was the most diligent employee at Toys "R" Us, working full-time hours, but I knew that even I had to aspire for more. So I enrolled at Adelphi University, only a ten-minute car ride from home. And Dad and I were ready to go car shopping with the money that I had saved.

New Rochelle Dodge was forty minutes away, assuming that traffic flowed uneventfully. The ride was heavy with worry, mostly mine, as I sat doing mental math to try to figure out what kind of car I could afford. We never discussed the finances, but Dad knew that I had amassed quite a significant amount of money from working, and I was ready to plop down a few thousand dollars as a deposit. His friend Art was the manager and would give us a deal.

The navy blue Omni seemed to stare at me, lonely and un-driven. Its front headlights were like eyes, and it was the most beautiful expression I had ever seen. We went in to the office to calculate the monthly payments I would be making based on the size of my down payment. It only took a few minutes to sign the paperwork, and we were on the road together, me following my father carefully on the expressway. The car had a glorious new upholstery smell, and as I drove, I glanced out the windows as though I was driving a Maserati. The fear of not being able to make the payments on a timely basis overtook my sense of elation. I would have to get another job.

Genovese Drug Store was the largest chain on Long Island, and I secured a job there with little effort. Toys R Us was played out and too far from my house. Genovese was conveniently located a couple of miles from Adelphi University in Garden City, and I was able to arrange my hours there around my school schedule. Working practically a full-time schedule, I was easily able to cover the cost of the car payments and the insurance premiums that my dad was expecting, as the insurance for my car remained in his name. It was cheaper.

The scale continued to be a part of my morning routine. Stretch first. Then weigh myself. Shower. Blow hair and apply makeup. When I was fully dressed, I was allowed to eat. There was little, if any, deviation from this ritual. My sense of self became intertwined with the number on that scale. I was up to a scary 140.

Despite the semester that I took off, I was still ahead of the game because of the college credits that I took in high school. I surely did not want to be behind anyone; it was bad enough that I had to justify my return from Rutgers. Commuting to a local school like Adelphi certainly wasn't prestigious, but it would do for now.

Classes were interesting enough, even on the easy side, and I declared myself a foreign language major in Spanish and French. The highlight of my day was the Ballet for Non-Majors class twice a week at 2:00 p.m. Mr. Hightorn, a professional dancer in his late sixties, taught the class every Tuesday and Thursday. There was a live pianist whose music filled the high ceilings and spaces of the dance studio. As I climbed over the indoor track and caught sight of the ballet barre, I was carried into a world of beautiful bodies and graceful movements that I dreamed of belonging to. As my dance classes endured, so did my hunger, which occupied every tendu, plier, and pirouette.

I would eye the university cafeteria with desire each and every time I entered. *Look at all of those out-of-shape students. So young and clearly not watching their calorie intake.* Being so accustomed to the sensations of starvation, I eyed the various culinary treats and almost tasted them in my mind. There was no room for self-indulgence. There had to be a male somewhere on campus that would spot me, as long as I maintained physical flawlessness.

Edgardo was an undergraduate student from Columbia. He was a well-dressed and suave Latino, with a sexy accent. He began chatting with me during my second semester in the cafeteria as I sat alone, grabbing a limited number of calories before heading off to Spanish class. It was interesting to learn about the sugar company that his family owned back home. Of course he was shorter than me. But that didn't seem to bother him as much as it did me, as he seemed to be a fixture in the dining hall every time I found myself there. The only one who was troubled was Evelyn, his fiancée, who was born in New York. After she caught sight of us one day and gave me a look, he stopped talking to me. Convinced that I had done something wrong, I made sure to avoid making eye contact with him after that. He stopped coming to the cafeteria.

Suzy, one of the students in my dance class, was drop-dead gorgeous. Blonde. I tried to stare at her as she entered the class only when I knew she wasn't looking. Beautiful body and smart outfits. Soon after the classes began that fall semester, a good-looking guy would wait for her at the entrance of the gym building and give her a hug and messy kiss. I often walked by and imagined what it would feel like to be noticed by a boy. Any boy. He was probably only interested in blondes, anyway.

As the first two semesters passed swiftly, so did my time. Nerves filled every moment of my day. Reprieve came only as I entered the phone booth on the first floor of the university center and called Dr. Rendall. She said that I could call if I was having difficulty making it to the end of the day, and I was between sessions. It would have been so much simpler if cell phones were accessible so I could have had more privacy, instead of being out in the open and feeling exposed and vulnerable to the world's judgments and disapproval. As I plopped a continuous stream of small coins into the phone, Dr. Rendall questioned my state of mind and the reason for my call. As other students passed by, I managed to squeak out a phony smile behind the folding glass doors. To Dr. Rendall, I was able to convey my feelings of inadequacy and hunger. As I spilled my feelings, I often heard her chewing on her lunch. I thought that was inconsiderate of my feelings and physical deprivation of nourishment. She did not seem engrossed any longer in what I had to say, even when I went to see her in person, and I caught her yawning many times during my visits. It was as if I was a hamster on a running wheel, saying the same words over and over again. I was grateful for her help at a critical time, and she got me talking about food, which probably saved my life. I realized that I needed another therapist.

CHAPTER TWELVE

The psychologist from the special needs school where my mother worked as a teacher, and later as an administrator, recommended Kara. Mom had finished her bachelor's degree and had gone on for her degree in administration and was quickly moving up the ranks in education. This was quite an accomplishment for her generation, and I was regularly the focal point of her studies and research projects when she needed to observe childhood behaviors and motivations. Michael Sykes spoke highly of Kara and insisted that she would be of great assistance to me, particularly at what he claimed was the best time in my life to go through whatever it was that I was going through. Clearly she was not as wise as he thought, especially since she told my father that I was a strong, young woman after he drove me to my very first visit at eighteen. I thought she was full of shit and that she probably said that to all of her new patients to get them to like and trust her.

My standing appointment was every Tuesday, at 6:30 p.m., and after that initial visit with Dad, I drove myself. I was able to afford her fee of ninety-five dollars on my income from Genovese Drugs, supplemented by the occasional babysitting gig that I still got called for. Once the second door of her office closed and I was whisked into her therapy room, I could feel my anxiety float out of my body, usually on a river of tears. Fortunately, she offered an endless supply of tissues on the small table directly to the left of the couch that I found myself on for years. Kara sat only a few feet away from me on a natural wood rocking chair, with a soft blue cushion that cradled her as she initiated the conversation each week.

We started by getting to know each other. It took months. I was still taking the prescribed dosage of Ludiomil that Dr. Rendall had recommended, and Kara questioned the need for me to continue that regimen. "Do you really want to be taking medication indefinitely? How do you feel about stopping that for now and focusing on exploring your childhood and the roots of what brought you here?" I wanted so badly to believe her. All I wanted was a hug of reassurance, but I wasn't sure if therapists were allowed to do that. So I held off. And I stopped taking the medication.

Week after week, I landed on that spongy couch, crying into tissue after tissue. At times, my tears would start in the car on my way over. It didn't take much to set me off. There were songs that were just too painful to listen to on the radio, but I never understood why they got to me. Depression was like a permanent cloud above my head, following me everywhere and always looming. Kara always greeted me and said good-bye with a pleasant smile and gentle voice. Sometimes I could hear her husband's heavy footsteps in the staircase of her house, adjacent to her office. I often wondered what he was like and what it felt like to be loved, as I am sure she was. And then there were the books that called out their names from the bookshelves lining the room. Topics ranged from childhood depression to adolescent aggression and family dysfunction. I bet she had read each and every one of them.

It was nearly a year until I was able to get past the crying and into talking about myself as a child. Not that I didn't cry often, but it did not overtake my session, and I became capable of exploring feelings that had been suppressed. Recollections of kindergarten and school were the first ones that came to mind. As I detailed the anxiety, vulnerability, and loneliness, I became that child again, putting to words the pain that I had desperately locked away for so many years.

"So tell me about your family," she stated after she had intently listened to my inner child verbalize for the first time.

I was able to begin opening up about my shyness and fear of other people, including family members. "Most of the time, I was stuck to my mom's side like glue," I explained. And then I remembered how she used to explain to people that I was like a plug in her side, connected at all times. She said it with a smile of satisfaction. If I wasn't alone, I was with her, and that just felt like where I was expected to be. I was called the "sensitive one," and she seemed to enjoy me needing her and being by her side. But when she and I weren't together, I was isolated and scared. Kara asked me if there were any other relationships that I had in the family. I answered no.

Incapable of connecting to my feelings, there were times when I drew a blank and could not respond to her probing. The sense of frustration was overpowering. Kara would rephrase her questions until she could squeeze some reaction from me. In my dreams, however, I was able to demonstrate a stronger voice and resolve certain situations that seemed impossible to negotiate. In one dream, I was packing my bags and leaving the home that I grew up in. Not many bags at all, kind of like a large carry-on. Nobody was around, but there was a blonde woman in the downstairs bathroom. She was putting on her eye shadow, in a series of pastel colors. She would not show me how to apply it, even as I stared at her through what seemed like a bakery window, salivating. As I got to the living room door to leave, I took one last look around. Silence.

There were other dreams where I was able to speak up to my sisters, demanding to know why they were treating me that way and ignoring my mere existence. I did all of the talking; they never responded. And still other dreams where I became that beautiful girl, heads turning everywhere. It took years to recognize the healing power of these dreams and to analyze them with Kara to move forward in my life.

But the dreadful ones often overshadowed these. Ones in which I was drowning or falling. Dying but still alive. Others where I was being chased endlessly, overwhelmed with fear, but never caught. And many filled with fear that terrible things would happen to my family because of me.

As in real life, I was often unable to voice my inner child during the dream experience, but Kara guided my interpretation and helped me to use the imagery as a springboard for my emotional healing. All of the things that I hoped for—confronting my sisters, standing up for myself, and being attractive—were buried in my subconscious. In my dreams, Kara explained, I was fulfilling my hopes and getting in touch with my anger. I resented the fact that I was not noticed, never told how I looked, and that the dynamics with my sisters were not addressed. Sigmund Freud claimed that the content of dreams represented "wish fulfillment." Carl Jung, whose theories of analytical psychology Kara studied in great depth, stated that dreams were compensations of the underdeveloped part of the psyche.

As the years went by, and as those inner doors of pain were pried open, I found myself becoming more and more frightened and even dreaming more about my death. Whenever I began to experience Dr. Rendall's rays of sunshine, little bursts of happiness, and pleasure in life, it petrified me. I did not want to get overly comfortable with those new feelings of pleasure and joy, in case they were short-lived. According to Kara, I was apprehensive because I did not feel worthy of or entitled to them. Her clinical term for this stage in my therapy was Generalized Anxiety Disorder, characterized by extreme worrying and disproportionate anxiety about several aspects of my life. This uneasiness lasted for five years.

There was one thing that I was sure of, and I was able to express this to Kara. Besides my own dog, I had always wanted a big brother. Either one of these could have been an ally, protected me, looked up to me, or thought I was special. Growing up with mostly females in the house, relating to boys was an unknown. There was a definite amount of mystery to the opposite sex. Though my father was a physical presence in the house, I never felt that I was good enough, and he was not attentive enough to reassure me otherwise. I can recall only one gift that he ever gave me, and that was a colorful, plastic link bracelet, though I am still unsure how old I was at the time. As I aged, I can remember him telling me that I had it more together than my sisters, but still, I assumed that I was doing something wrong, that I needed to work harder and change myself to win his approval. "No, I don't remember anyone ever telling me that I was pretty," I answered Kara.

Kara discussed the therapeutic term of mirroring. Parental mirroring, I learned, provides the child with the basis for a healthy sense of self.

The basis of healthy self-esteem is that one's natural self, with all its emotions, with its successes and failures, is acceptable and lovable. If the child does not feel his parents love him for himself, apart from accomplishments, he will develop what object relations theorists call the "false self," the self that is fabricated in order to get the approval of his parents, based on the ability to achieve good grades, a good job, a good mate, etc.

Kara began giving me articles and books to read. She started with *Tales from Moominvalley: The Story of the Invisible Child,* by Tove Jansson, a Finnish author. The main character, Ninny, was disregarded and lost all sense of self, going into hiding. She had no voice. Ninny did not know how to play or even how to laugh until she had some definition, until she truly existed. She was able to find her true self. I wasn't sure what Ninny and I had in common, but somehow I felt sorry for her. She was all alone.

Alice Miller's *The Drama of the Gifted Child: The Search for the True Self* came next. Miller speaks of hiding feelings, needs, and memories. I inhaled every word of her book:

One weapon we have … is the emotional discovery of the truth about the unique history of our childhood. This path, although certainly not easy, is the only route by which we can at last leave behind the cruel, invisible prison of our childhood. We become free by transforming ourselves from unaware victims of the past into responsible individuals in the present, who are aware of our past and are thus able to live with it.

Kara began speaking of a repressed pain that, so overwhelming, was at times replaced with achievement to avoid its fury. My accomplishments, academic and otherwise, filled a void within me, but it was never enough. I had no sense of self, and I was unable to put my feelings to words. I said practically nothing as a child, not wanting to be as demanding and challenging as Ellie. Sitting in Kara's office, at twenty-four, I could not muster up one of my own sentiments about who I was. Like an amoeba, I had no definition.

Over the years, as I began to unleash the hurt and become aware of the alienation of my own body, I allowed myself to grow my hair longer, from the boyish seventies "shag," as my father used to call it admiringly, to a risky midshoulder-length, feminine hairdo. With that came more formfitting clothes, though it took years for me to feel at ease wearing them. Then came the makeup. And the nails. I was still quite conservative in applying the colors and shades, but it felt good. I took it slow. No one paid attention. My hair lengthened at a rate of a quarter of an inch per year. Highlights at the hair salon came on at a snail's pace, too, beginning with the two front strands. What I thought was completely over the top was barely noticeable. Clothes were still shapeless, as my appetite had increased, and I was determined to cover up my growing body that scared the crap out of me. I was capable of sporting a dress from time to time, provided it was not too clingy. I was ashamed of how I looked and was constantly adjusting my clothes to make sure that nothing was out of place. My self-loathing was unwavering, but it was a start. I never wore a bathing suit.

After I graduated from Adelphi University, one year early, I got my first job as an administrative assistant in Manhattan. The job was easy to come by in the late eighties, when college graduates had their pick, and I happened to be in the employment agency when the call came in from Chanel for a bilingual French-speaking assistant to the CFO of the New York office. Making a real salary, even entry level, delighted me. Commuting on the train, I had twelve-hour days, from the time I took the 7:15 a.m. into Penn Station, until the moment I set foot in the door at 7:00 p.m.

Appointments with Kara were hard to keep, so she suggested that I come see her at 6:00 a.m., park my car in front of her house, and walk to the train station a couple of blocks away. Fortunately I was a morning person, because I had to leave my house at 5:15 a.m. Kara would be sipping her tea, and I would be mindful of the time, always ticking away rapidly. In a blink, she gave me the five-minute warning, and I was on my way to the train by foot. I made sure that my makeup bag was with me as my eye makeup, though minimal, had to be reapplied, unless I remembered to wear the waterproof mascara to repel the tears. Often, I dozed on the train until I heard the announcement that we had arrived at Penn.

One morning, more than six years into therapy, I could not get to my appointment. I just was not able to get going that day. The house was silent, as it usually was when I readied myself to leave the house for my visit, often in the dark, depending on the season. My legs felt lethargic, though I was not physically ill. I was suspended in midair. I called Kara and told her I could not make it, and even though I rarely cancelled an appointment, especially last minute, I was hesitant.

"What is it that you do not want to face today?" she asked over the phone, as I attempted to explain that I was not going to make my scheduled time. With a knot in my stomach, I choked on a response, which never came out. Powerless to explain myself, I realized that there were many times that I left therapy in pain that stayed with me until the next session, lingering heavily on my mind. The following week, Kara brought this issue up as my buttocks hit the couch. I started to cry, not wanting to disappoint her. For the life of me, it was impossible to describe why I had to cancel that morning. Holding on to my own perception was out of the question. Kara was omnipotent and all-knowing. I was clearly in the wrong, and I made sure that I never missed another appointment. Even if I was not feeling up to it.

In my midtwenties, I started to get noticed by the opposite sex. I still felt ugly but was more equipped to maintain a superficial conversation. I became attached to each man that paid attention to me, not that they were waiting in lines in front of my house. Like Guy, the handsome doctor, doing his residency at a Brooklyn hospital. When he asked me to dance one night out with my friends, I looked behind me to make sure he was not talking to someone else. Guy asked me out, but I got sick from shellfish on our first date, which I discovered later I was deathly allergic to. We dated for a couple of months, and I met his sister and her husband, which was a sure sign that he was the one.

He was nice enough, really cute, first kiss and all, but clearly was not interested in a long-term relationship. On each date, I was spilling over with insecurities about my appearance and how to apply my makeup without looking like a clown. Doubts were there at every turn, though he did not pick up on them, and I always worried about what he thought of me. Guy was charming and took me out to dinner often. I knew I had to convince him to feel the same way I did. Driving to the hospital where he lived and worked, I looked in the rearview mirror every two minutes to see if I looked presentable. On my drive over, the minutes passed torturously slow until I arrived. I lived for that moment.

Guy stopped calling after about six months. I was devastated. Kara explained to me that he just had different intentions and that his medical career came first. Deep down I knew that I was not good enough, not pretty enough, not intelligent enough. We continued to focus our sessions on those ways of thinking and behaving, and on my low self-esteem.

When Farjad winked at me at the dance club about a year later, in 1987, I nearly fell off my seat. Again, I did a quick 360-degree glance to be sure another woman was not directly behind me who he had his eyes on. He then approached and began talking to me. It didn't really matter what he had to say; he was actually speaking to me. And I melted right then and there.

Farjad and I dated for a couple of years. As in kindergarten, I hoped to be more beautiful, smarter, and more loved than any other woman in his life. His mother did not speak to me and never once made eye contact when I was in her home. Born in Tehran, Farjad and his family never assimilated to the American culture and maintained a family environment of traditional Persian values.

Farjad's father was the only one in the family who acknowledged my presence, possibly because he shared Jewish roots on his grandfather's side, he explained. He was friendly and warmhearted, especially to his mistress. His attention gave me false hope that I could win the rest of the family over. Though I tried to be Persian, dress the part, cook traditional Basmati rice and stew, and even learn Farsi, it was never enough. And Farjad had a wandering eye for other women, which added to my insecurities about how I looked. I worked so hard to be more beautiful, at least what he measured to be so, but it was never sufficient.

In the meantime, I had been searching for an apartment that I could afford and was able to rent out the basement of an elderly couple living in Elmont, on the border of Queens. The commute into the Big Apple was shortened, and when Farjad came over, I made sure to have some of his favorite foods. The couple across the hall always knew that I was preparing something different, and they let me know that the aroma filled the entire level of the house. They referred to me as the "upset girl," and Michelle was frequently the sounding board for my tears of disappointment with Farjad. When I showed my neighbor the pieces of jewelry from his family's shop in the city that he had presented to me, she grimaced, though with admiration. I did not share with her that I had to pay for part of them.

Farjad's family spent every weekend practicing Islam at a mosque in Queens. Many times I drove him to the mosque, but I never dared to go inside. Farjad did not ask me to, so I would sit in the car for hours waiting for him. Alone. I shared with Kara that all I required was to be in his presence and win his affection. As in the time I went with him to the animal shelter to get a dog for his family. "Shah," as he named it, was a young, black Labrador retriever, and we played with it endlessly the first day he was home. Shah disappeared a few days later, and Farjad hinted that his father let him go but had no explanation of how he went missing. It didn't add up. Shah was never seen again, and I was heartbroken about what I had allowed to happen.

I watched as his close friend Mohammad, married to American Linda, began to expect her to completely conform to the Persian way of life. Though they were married and lived in Manhattan, she gave up herself completely to him in every way. Linda wore customary Iranian garb, cooked his favorite meals, and stopped seeing her own family to gratify him. One summer, the four of us flew to Greece on vacation. Farjad seemed grateful that I had paid for our airline tickets. I was still jealous of Linda and the fact that Mohammad committed to her, and I put all of my energy into conforming.

This hunger for attention never subsided, for I was acknowledged only as his American "whore," whose days with him were numbered until he would marry his preselected traditional wife. It was a challenge to acknowledge the vast cultural differences that would never allow for him and his family to accept and care for me the way I needed. My father named him the "terrorist," an eerie premonition of what was to come on September 11, 2001, although no one in my family actually knew the circumstances of my relationship with Farjad. The crushing rejection by Farjad and his family hit a familiar nerve. With Kara's support, I was at last able to begin to articulate my sense of worthlessness. "Will I ever be loved and worshipped by any man?" I asked. It was a yearning that was incessant. I broke it off with Farjad but was never sure it was the right move and frequently saw him as the last chance for a man in my life.

Over the next year after the breakup, Kara and I focused on my ability to be alone. The first order of business was to analyze, feeling by feeling and body part by body part, what I liked and disliked about myself. The negative certainly outweighed the positive, but at least there was something upbeat for the first time. I enjoyed my longer hair and some of the styles that I was allowing myself to indulge in. It was hard to admit. My sense of self began to have some definition.

Post-Farjad, I took baby steps and began socializing with my college friends, hitting the dance clubs and going out to dinner, without a date, and attempting to be comfortable in my own skin. This meant wearing feminine clothes that I did not feel self-conscious in, just for my own satisfaction. Over the next several months, I enjoyed my own company. And I laughed for the first time—a real, wholehearted laugh—at the age of twenty-six. I was at a club with some friends, and they were making jokes about our friend Cal, and how he had difficulty picking up social cues. When a woman clearly did not want to interact with him, he just kept on talking. We laughed until we cried and our sides hurt. I believe it's true that in order to truly laugh, one must know how to cry. Well, I did. Up until this point, I did not have a sense of humor and was too serious. Laughing represented a loss of control. I eyed the patrons around me to see if I was overly loud, but they were in their own worlds of banter and entertainment.

With the laughter came the realization that I had feelings, rights, and needs, although it would still take years for me to feel entitled to them. The human race finally welcomed me as a member, vulnerabilities and all. Perfectionism began to lose its appeal. It was a rebirth, a renaissance, and I was alive for the first time.

On December 22, 1989, I was waiting for my brother-in-law, Ian, to return home to his apartment in Queens with my car that he had borrowed. His holiday party went overtime, and he did not return home until close to midnight. I tried to back out of my plans with Roger, as my sweatpants seemed a much more comfortable option at that late hour. However, my friend from Adelphi insisted that I join him. Honestly, the laughter and fun appealed to me, and we went out to Brooklyn on the late side that Saturday night to a club named Bop She Bop. With a name like that, it was no surprise that the club greeted me with a sea of polyester and seventies disco music. At about two in the morning, I noticed a tall, good-looking man with a leather jacket stroll in the front door.

Eric strolled over to me as I was sitting at the bar, nursing my ginger ale. "Wow, you are tall," he said with a nervous smirk. Thinking him observant, I agreed, and we began talking. A couple of minutes into the conversation, Eric pulled out a picture of his infant daughter,

Amy. He explained how he was recently divorced but that he had a child. I admired his honesty. At the end of the night, he gave me his business card in the hopes that we could get together. I called him first since I did not have a phone installed in my new apartment in Forest Hills, and cell phones were not available.

We went out on the last day of 1989 on our first date. I was terrified about what to wear, so I stuck with the baggy pants and bulky sweater. There was a light snowfall. Eric picked me up in his gold, metallic Honda Civic, one that he described as a "cockroach," and he opened the door for me. He commented on how nice I looked, though he wondered why I hid myself with loose-fitting clothing. It was a comment that he continued to make during our dating. It was difficult to be gracious about compliments that I was hearing for the first time.

As we strolled down the street, disturbing the coating of snow that was accumulating on the sidewalk on our way to dinner, he reached out and held my hand. Uncomfortable, I was anxious and unsure of how hard to hold his hand, and if I should squeeze or leave it limp. But I did not want to let go, as uncertain as I felt. He treated me to dinner, and we toasted 1990 at a local party. A caring kiss on the cheek ended the night, a first for me at twenty-six.

Kara and I analyzed my feelings about Eric and how he made me feel. I told her how I filled up with emotion when he said I was beautiful, crying often. I even doubted him and thought that he was just saying that at first. That he did not really mean it. His attention was smothering. Kara helped me to understand my sense of unworthiness and how Eric's words created anxiety within me. She was confident that he was sincere and agreed with him.

Eric and I dated for three years, with just as many breakups. He was terrified of getting married again after his first, awful run of it. And I was just as petrified of being abandoned. My fears got in the way just as much as his. The last time we split up, he showed up at my door, with tears in his eyes, after about three months of separation. I didn't want to let him in my life again, but seeing a grown man cry was tough. And he must have been feeling something, Kara and I discussed.

A month later, Eric proposed. My father made his doubts known, particularly after the breakups along the way, and was inclined not to trust him. His negative comments made it less fun to be newly engaged. But we pushed forward, confidence issues and all. I gave up my apartment and moved into his once there was a ring on my finger. We were married on March 21, 1993, in a mildly Jewish ceremony, with a female rabbi. Remnants of my eating disorder remaining, I felt chubby in my wedding dress, which was a size-ten sample from the famous Kleinfelds in Brooklyn. I managed to put it on with a smile on my face, and I suppressed those feelings of anxiety and insecurity, not fitting in with the in-laws for the four-hour reception. Amy was our flower girl.

My first daughter, Amelia, was born a year later. Through therapy, I had learned how to eat again and began to nourish my body and mind. There was another life inside of me, dependent on me, and I made sure that I nourished that one as well. She was born on October 23, 1994, a healthy eight pounds, seven ounces. Her sister, Emma, arrived on August 15, 1996, and Daniel on May 25, 1998. Three healthy babies in a matter of six years. My father asked if we ever watched TV.

Kara and I talked about the guilt feelings that I had in relation to my sisters. Ellie had difficulty getting pregnant, and Amelia was the first grandchild. Mazzy was not married, not even in a relationship. At one point, she passed along a comment from her friend who said, "Who would have thought that Leslie would have been the fertile one?" Kara pointed out that sense of entitlement again. I wasn't sure that it was acceptable to be the youngest of the siblings and the first to achieve these milestones. Kara assured me that it was and that I should bask in the happy, fulfilling moments that I was experiencing. I did love being a mother.

After the birth of my children, I saw a different, happier side of my father. It was the father that I saw on stage performing, truly enjoying life. He lit up each time he was with them. There were parts of his personality that I had never seen before, filled with hugs, laughter, tears, and all of the wonderful parts of being a grandpa. I wish that I could have seen them sooner, but I took them in like a sponge. And my children bathed in his affection. Mom was the typical, doting grandmother and was at our new house in Baldwin as often as she could be. Having children made me realize how much I had learned from her and what a loving parent she was.

My sisters, particularly Mazzy, took on a close relationship with my children. I continued to work in the city and to dance on the weekends, and she and my mother came often to babysit. The children's accomplishments were big news in my family, but mine seemed overlooked. I forged ahead with my graduate studies, despite Ellie's remark that I was "crazy" to be going to school. Kara saw this as envy and urged me not to count on their support or praise for my endeavors but rather to learn to do that for myself. Although discouraged, I managed to earn an MBA from Fordham University in six years.

After working fourteen-hour days, it was time to make a professional change. Eric had his own retail business with his family in Brooklyn, and one of us needed to be closer to home. I walked away from a corporate salary to return to school, once again, and study education. He was terrified, and this was unsettling, but I knew on some level that it would end up being the right move. It was hard to be patient with four young children to support and a mortgage.

One afternoon, a year into my studies and ten days after the September 11 terrorist attacks, my mother called me at about one o'clock in the afternoon, saying that she could not reach my father. She was at work, by then the principal of her school, and my father was typically at home, after an early lunch at the local greasy spoon, having run errands in the morning. My mother sounded concerned but refused my offer to ride over to the house in West Hempstead to check on him. She said she would leave work early and go home. I had an uneasy feeling but returned to my books, with another ninety minutes before I had to pick up the kids at school.

The phone rang again, about thirty minutes later. It was a female officer from the precinct close to my childhood home, who was with my mother. She explained that there had been an explosion at the house and that I needed to rush over as quickly as possible. When I asked if my father was all right, she simply responded that I needed to hurry but to be careful when driving. I hung up the phone, and my heart was racing. I didn't panic.

I scooped up the children and piled them into our suburban minivan. West Hempstead was about twenty minutes away, but it felt like the ride was five hours long. As I pulled down Madison Avenue, I was struck by yellow police tape framing the perimeter of the house and the front lawn. My stomach dropped, and as I approached the first line of police officers guarding the end of the block, I rolled down the window and explained that it was my house they were protecting. They said nothing but let me through.

When I arrived, the neighbor from across the street, whose children I had babysat, scurried to my car and took the children immediately into her house, with Buster, my father's dog. At that point, my mother came running to me, arms open wide, crying. It was at that point that I learned the dreadful truth of my father's death: there had been an oil burner explosion that morning, and my father died shortly after. My mother discovered his lifeless body in the bathroom, with Buster by his side. To this day, it is not clear whether he died from carbon monoxide fumes or a heart attack from the stress of the explosion, but the dog found one foot of clean air on the floor next to him and survived. He was not alone.

As I approached the side patio of the house, I saw a blue blanket with a small American flag emblem covering his limp body. He was fully covered, but one finger from his right hand managed to sneak out and stand upright, stiff with rigor mortis. It is a sight that I will never forget. We buried him quickly, that being the Jewish way in death and mourning. It was the only time I practiced Judaism.

I was about an hour late to the first visit to Kara after my father's accident, about one week later. It wasn't that I left any later than usual, but I got lost. I couldn't think straight, and it was impossible to remember anything clearly. She said she understood. I sat on her couch in a daze. I realized that I never told my father that I loved him. We talked for an extra hour, and she was certain that he knew and that in some way I was his favorite. Months later, I was able to remember a moment when he said I had it "all together" and that I was so tough that he was afraid of me. To this day, I hold on to these memories, though my time with my father was cut short.

CHAPTER THIRTEEN

I spent twenty years with Kara, until the day that she decided to retire to Florida. She started to plant the seeds of her departure several months before, but I never allowed myself to mention the agony and distress that it caused me, even just the thought of it. And she never asked. Thanks to Kara, I did not end up six feet under the ground. Kara used to say that I would share the things that I learned with my own children. These were gifts, she would add, that I would pass down to them. She was right. I enjoy every single second of being a mother, and I remind my daughters and son that they are light-years ahead of me at their age. More confident and less afraid of life. Talk about paying it forward.

The loss of my father drove a deeper wedge between my sisters and me, as he was not around to be a buffer between my mother, the unresolved sibling rivalries, and the petty nonsense. Over time, because of her own loss, she became closer to them, and they became increasingly heavy-handed with her time. Though our relationship has taken a hit, she is an astonishing woman who has taught me a great deal about raising children and being an educator. I needed to separate from her in order to grow and reach my full potential. We are learning to come back together in a healthier way, with love and respect. My sisters remain stuck in adolescence, repeating childhood patterns and dynamics. It is my hope that they will be able to grow up one day.

Perhaps then we can start a relationship, as adults, with admiration for each other's talents and differences.

On that last day in therapy, in the spring of 2002, Kara gave me a hug as I got up off of her couch. It was warm and enveloping, but I did not cry. Neither did she. She gave me her telephone number and address in Florida and said that I should feel free to contact her if I needed to. As I walked out of her room, I turned my head and took a last look. The hydrangea bushes greeted me again, but this time it was a farewell. As I started the engine, I took in the last image of her safe and charming cornflower-yellow cottage. It was the last time I saw her.

I was thirty-nine, with a family of my own. My journey with Kara had come to an end. She had taught me how to feel worthy of love, food, and attention. Unlike the eighteen-year-old who showed up at her office, I got out of bed without anxiety. I was dancing still, but for the pure joy of it. I graduated and began teaching children from other countries how to speak English, children who had no voices. I had hopes and dreams for a fulfilled life. That bedroom door was finally closed. Kara was right: I was strong.